WITHDRAWN

FALL
FROM
GRACE

ALSO BY CHARLES BENOIT

Relative Danger

Out of Order

Noble Lies

You

CHARLES BENOIT

FALL

FROM

GRACE

HARPER TEEN

An Imprint of HarperCollinsPublishers

Library of Congress Cataloging-in-Publication Data
Benoit, Charles.
Fall from Grace / Charles Benoit. — 1st ed.
    p. cm.
Summary: Inspired by an intriguing girl who is nothing like his
shallow girlfriend, a high school senior whose life has been mapped
out by his parents makes some surprising decisions that lead him to
take dangerous—but exhilarating—risks.
ISBN 978-0-06-194707-0
[1. Conduct of life—Fiction. 2. Choice—Fiction. 3. Interpersonal
relations—Fiction. 4. Stealing—Fiction. 5. High schools—Fiction.
6. Schools—Fiction.] I. Title.
PZ7.B447114Fal 2012   2011026148
[Fic]—dc23   CIP
                                                             AC

Typography by Andrea Vandergrift
12 13 14 15 16   LP/RRDH   10 9 8 7 6 5 4 3 2 1

First Edition

To Rose, my partner in crime.

"It's the tie. I had to wear one."

She reached up and gave it a tug. "At least it's not a clip-on." It wasn't, but it might as well have been. His father had tied it for him months ago and each time he wore it, he slipped it off over his head, hanging it on the hook on the back of his bedroom door, the misshapen knot pulled too tight to untangle. "So, you gonna get me that treaty?"

"What do you need it for?"

"Do you really care?"

"I might."

"You don't. It's a make-believe treaty written by a bunch of high school students pretending to be the ambassadors of real countries they couldn't find on a map. Picking a theme for the senior prom has more global impact."

That wasn't the way Mr. Jansen had explained Model United Nations, but so far it was the most accurate description he'd heard. He had joined late in the quarter, too late to know what he was supposed to be doing, but, as his mother had pointed out, not too late to add it to his college application. She said he needed an extracurricular activity, something academic, that he could list along with all the volunteer work his parents had arranged for him to do. His father would have preferred that he join Public Speaking, but that would have meant speaking in public, and as determined as they were on getting him into a good school, even his parents couldn't get around that. That's why they settled on MUN. He was just glad they didn't know there was a chess club.

"I've been to this school before," Grace said, looking past the open gym doors and down the long corridor. "There's a photocopier in the teachers' lounge. I'll have it back in five minutes, tops."

"If you think this whole thing is stupid—"

"And I do, but go on."

"—why do you want the treaty?"

"*I* don't want it, the US team wants it. I'm cutting a little deal on the side. I get them the details of the treaty, they give me North Dakota."

"Why would you want North Dakota?"

"It would complete the set. Look, you going to get it for me or not?"

"If I don't, what happens then?"

"Then we both have to think of something to do to fill up the four hours before this ridiculous event is over."

He could think of plenty of things they could do for four hours, and if he were that kind of guy, the put-it-out-there kind who was smooth with the words and fast with the ladies, they'd be off in some empty classroom, getting busy. He wasn't, not even close, but that didn't stop him from thinking about it. Besides, Zoë would find out for sure and she'd be pissed and she'd tell his mother because they were tight like that and then he'd hear about it from his parents, plus he'd have to see Zoë—and all of Zoë's friends—every day in school, and he could guess what that would be like. Nope, even if he was that kind of guy it wasn't worth it. Still, for an uncontrolled, hormone-driven second, he thought about it.

"Four hours at a MUN event is a long, long time," she said. "If you don't help get the treaty. I'll be so bored I'll probably declare war on Luxembourg and then you'll have that on your conscience."

He weighed the pretend global consequences before nodding. "Anything for world peace. Wait here, I'll go get it."

"Hold it." She grabbed his wrist and pulled him back, stronger than she looked. Her hand was cool and dry against his skin. "You just can't walk up and take it."

"Yes I can. There're copies on the table, I'll get one and—"

"We have to have a plan first. And signals and code words and a Plan B and an escape route...."

"How about this for a plan? I go get it and give it to you."

"Oh, come on. You're taking all the fun out of it."

"You *are* bored. Okay, what's the plan?"

The metal bleachers were pushed closed against the wall, but someone had pulled out a couple rows at the bottom where delegates from around the make-believe world had tossed their book bags and winter coats. She led him to an open section and took a seat, flipping to a blank page in a notebook that wasn't hers.

"We'll call it Operation Trick-or-Treat."

"Because you like Halloween?"

"No, because I like taking candy from babies." She wrote the words at the top of the paper in blocky capital letters. She drew a quick map of the gym and the hallway. "Next, we need code names. I'll be Al'ea and you can be Bix."

"Bix? What kind of name is Bix?"

She looked at him, stunned by his ignorance. "Al'ea

and Bix? From *Reality Frat House*?"

Blank stare.

"You're kidding, right? They're *famous*."

"Famous for what?"

"For being famous, geez, what do you think? They're on TV, that's all they have to do." She shook her head and mumbled as she continued to map out the room. "I can't believe you don't know who Bix is."

"How about calling me Sawyer?"

"Which Sawyer? The one from *Random Roommates* or the one from *Spring Break Survival*?"

"The one from East High School."

"That's your name? Sawyer?" She gave him the quick up and down. "No, it doesn't fit. Let's go with Bix. But just for this job."

"Good. It would be a pain to have to get my driver's license changed."

She focused on the paper, drawing arrows one way, erasing them and going another, the tip of her tongue sticking out between her lips as she made the simple complex. He leaned forward, elbows on his knees, and waited. Nothing else to do. The North Korean team— his team—were bent over their laptops, finalizing the resolutions he wasn't allowed to help with. Well, he *could* if he *really* wanted to, but it's just that it's so *late* in the process and the team had already *done* all the background work and he'd have *so far* to go to catch up and he could still play an important role, sure, but not with the writing or the presenting or the debates, definitely not the debates, but sorta like a goodwill ambassador, that way he could get to know how the event works so next time he can play a bigger role—well not *next* time, since that's the regionals, but after that, maybe. They were sure he understood.

"All right, we're here," Grace said, tapping two small Xs with the point of her pencil. "Here's North Korea, and right next to it is Denmark. I'll go to the Denmark table, and I'll make something up about how they should join Belgium in blocking imports from countries with dictatorships. That'll get your team all hot and bothered. Meanwhile, you come around like this, between Kuwait and Kyrgyzstan. Wait by Trinidad. When you hear me say 'Why do you think they call them *dic*tators,' you grab the paper, then make your way over to Singapore and leave the paper behind those blue mats. I'll head to Mexico. Give me the sign when you've planted the paper and I'll go pick it up."

"What sign is that?"

"Ever see *The Sting*?" She held up a finger and tapped it along the side of her nose.

"Another reality show?"

"You don't know *The Sting*? What do they teach you over at East?" She shook her head some more. "I'll pick up the paper, take it down to the teachers' lounge, and burn a copy. It would be easier to just take a picture of it, but the US team has crappy phones so they need a hard copy. I'll put the original back by the mats, then you put it back in the folder. Easy." She folded the paper and stuck it in her jeans, dropping the pencil in the pocket of his shirt. "Now, you ready for this?"

CHAPTER

AS SOON AS he opened his locker, Sawyer knew someone had gone through it.

Things had been rearranged, not a lot but enough
to notice—notebooks that he always kept on the floor
were on the shelf, the paperbacks were lined up by size,
his spare hoodie moved from the right hook to the left,
the magnetic mirror moved halfway down the inside of
the door.

The first person that came to mind was Zoë.

Two years ago, before they started enforcing the
no-sharing-lockers rule, she had used his locker as a
dumping ground for the things she didn't want to carry
or as overflow storage when her locker was too trashed

to cram in any more. But that all changed after the knife incident at West High, and now the administration viewed using someone else's locker as a Homeland Security violation. Besides, his locker wasn't anywhere near Zoë's classes and she had enough trouble remembering her own combination, let alone his. And if for some reason she *had* gone through his locker, she would never have left it so neat.

There was always the chance that it had been security guards looking for drugs. They'd never checked lockers before, but that didn't mean they couldn't start. Not that they would have found anything—not that they'd even think of him as the type of kid to bring drugs to school—but as he tried to figure out who'd been in his locker, the security guards were an option.

Then he saw the paper bag in the back corner. It was the same size bag you'd get if you bought a liter of Mountain Dew, and even with the top of the bag scrunched closed, he knew there was a bottle inside. He also knew he hadn't put it there.

Sawyer knelt down and moved in closer. He made a show of moving some books around, flipping through binders for a paper he was wasn't looking for, and when there was a lull in traffic, he reached into the top of the bag and felt the pointed teeth of a bottle cap.

Someone had left him a beer.

If Dillon had been in town and if they were still close, Sawyer would have assumed it was him. But since Dillon wasn't in town and they weren't close, Sawyer kept thinking. If he felt the tapered neck of a wine cooler or the smooth metal sides of a Bacardi O twist-off, he would have thought Zoë. But it was beer, and beer wasn't Zoë. It could have been a setup, the kind of prank assholes did to get somebody suspended, putting alcohol into someone's locker and tipping off the administration. He'd never heard of it happening at East, but he could be the first.

Crouched in tight, Sawyer inched the dark brown bottle from the bag.

Duvel Belgian golden ale.

Taped to the back of the bottle was a note:

WELL DONE, 007.
CHEERS,
G

Sawyer moved quick, putting the bottle back in the bag, laying the bag on its side, then stacking books around it to keep it hidden.

It would be hours before he'd have a chance to sneak it into his backpack and out of the school, and he knew he'd be sweating the entire time. He never did anything wrong, and it would be just his luck to get busted the very first time. What the hell was this girl Grace thinking? And how'd she get in his locker in the first place, or even known where his locker was? And what was she doing at East?

He moved the mirror back in place, and when he saw himself smiling he had to admit that, okay, okay, it *was* funny.

Stupid funny.

Just like at the MUN event.

She was right, he had been bored and he hadn't cared about the treaty and helping her steal it did make the day go by faster. It was stupid and immature and uncalled for and disrespectful and all that.

But it was fun.

His parents wouldn't think so, and Zoë would've gone ballistic if she knew he had spent the day conspiring with a Westie girl no matter *how* they met, but his parents didn't have to know and maybe he didn't have to tell Zoë everything.

As he closed his locker and headed to English class—late for the first time all year—Sawyer wondered what else Grace did for fun.

TWO WEEKS LATER, there she was again.

He was working the Sunday afternoon shift at Mike's Ice Cream, and if it were summer or if the sun had been out, it would have been busy, but nobody thinks *ice cream* when it's cold and wet and gray. Five, six customers since the shift started and there'd be maybe that many more before it was over. For the hundredth time he wiped down the spotless counter and tried to tune out the satellite radio permanently set to the '50s channel.

His father was in the same golf league as the owner, which is why Sawyer got the job and why he had to keep it. There were times, though, more now that the weather was crap and the four hours felt like four hundred, when he wondered what it would be like to quit and find a job on his own, something he actually enjoyed doing or that was at least a challenge. Then he'd think about what his parents would say and that would be the end of that.

He had finished with the counter and had moved on to the metal sink by the register where they kept the ice cream scoops when the reindeer bells on the back of the door rang and she walked in. The combat boots, the bright purple jacket zippered up tight against the red scarf, the two white wires leading out from under the black knit cap, that was all different, but the way he was pulled in by her eyes was the same.

He rearranged the scoops in the sink, careful not to let her catch him looking. He knew she knew, but that's the game and how it's played. And she played her part. He watched her reflection in the cooler window as she stuffed the hat in her pocket and pushed her hair behind her ears. An earbud dropped free and she left it dangling as she walked to the counter. He looked up and gave her the do-I-know-this-girl head tilt, followed by a hey-it's-you-again smile, trying to act like he wasn't acting.

She smiled too, with him or at him, he wasn't sure.

"The ice cream man," she said, leaning up against the counter. "Are all your flavors guaranteed to satisfy?"

"Except for the no-fat ones. Nobody likes those." He dropped a stray spoon in the sink and wiped his hands on his Mike's Ice Cream apron. "What brings you way over here?"

She took a step back and put up her hands in mock surprise. "Sorry, sheriff. Didn't know us no-account Westsiders weren't welcome in these here east parts."

"It's lousy out there," Sawyer said, pointing his chin toward the gray windows. "Far to go just for ice cream."

"I didn't come all this way for the ice cream," she said, looking at him as she said it, pausing as she leaned back in. "I came for the library."

"They've got one on the west side. By the Kmart."

"This one's twice the size and it's got a better law section." She looked past him to the board that listed forty-six flavors even though they didn't carry half that many. He watched those blue eyes dart along the rows of the names and watched her lips twitch as she read. He gave her time to work her way through them all, then said, "What do you want me to make you?"

17

"Famous. But for now just give me a small chocolate espresso ripple."

He wrapped a white napkin around the cone, then flipped open the curved glass case and scooped up a large serving. Bent over the tubs of ice cream, he could hear the tinny bass of her dangling earbud as she pressed against the glass. He offered sprinkles, she said no, she tried to give him a five but he wouldn't take it, telling her he was allowed to give away one free cone a day and she was it, a lie that worked for the both of them.

She tasted the ice cream. She could have done some long, slow lick thing, her tongue curling around the base of the scoop and working up slowly, *real* slowly, to the tip, all the while peeking out from under half-closed, smoky lashes, like Zoë and her friends would do when they were messing with him, acting all slutty just to get a rise out of him. But she didn't. She licked the ice cream like normal and that was it.

"Rancid," she said, running the back of her hand across her lips.

"Oh, sorry. Here, let me give you a new one."

"Not the ice cream. The band. It's Rancid. I saw your hand going with the beat, figured you'd want to know."

He didn't, but was impressed she had noticed one finger that barely moved.

"This is yummy. Thanks."

"The law stuff at the library. Is it for school?"

She shook her head and took a bite out of her ice cream, taking her time before answering. "No, something for me. Looking for loopholes."

"You could have looked it up online."

"I could've, but then no ice cream."

The pause, the clever comeback—she was done talking about it and he knew that, but he couldn't stop himself. "Did you find what you were looking for?"

Another pause. "Maybe. I'll let you know."

There was nothing left to talk about but he was in no hurry to see her go. Then he remembered his locker and said, "Oh yeah. Thanks for the beer."

"Thanks for North Dakota."

"How'd you know which locker was mine?"

She was focused on her ice cream and he thought she didn't hear the question, but then she said, "You'd be surprised what you can find online these days. And how simple it is to guess the password for your school's database. Seriously, the mascot's name? Please."

He was impressed. "They have the combination on there too?"

"Didn't need it."

"How'd you get in?"

"Family secret," she said, and winked as she said it.

Across the shop the bells jingled as a pack of Cub Scouts burst in and raced to the counter, followed by a pair of mothers who repeated ignored warnings about not running and using inside voices and not touching anything, apologizing in advance for the trouble they knew they brought with them.

Somewhere between the double-scoop cookie dough cone and the raspberry sundae, he noticed that Grace was gone.

CHAPTER

"I'LL GIVE YOU the same advice my father gave me."

Sawyer looked over to where his father was standing by the sink. It was close to ten at night and his father was brewing another cup of coffee. His parents loved the stuff, some genetic mutation that must have skipped a generation. Sawyer knew what advice was coming. It was the same advice he heard any time the topic came up, his father telling him that if he found a job he loved he'd never work a day in his life. It was a good line, better than the one about hard work being its own reward or how genius was 99 percent perspiration, but Sawyer had heard them all so many times he'd forgotten what they were trying to say.

"Find a job you love and you'll never work a day in your life."

"That's *so* true," his mother said, as if hearing it for the first time. She was sitting across from Sawyer at the kitchen table, reorganizing the color-coded folders where she kept the college brochures, financial-aid forms, letters of recommendation, and drafts of admission essays. "If you love what you're doing, it's not really work."

"Your mother's right. You never hear me complaining about my job."

Sawyer nodded along with his mother, thinking of all the times in the past month his father had gone on about his lazy coworkers or the ridiculous paperwork or the ungrateful clients or the rip-off suppliers or the clueless regional directors or the incompetent management team that was driving the company straight into the ground.

"Oh sure, it's not the most exciting job," his father said, waiting as the last of the coffee dripped into the pot, "but what job is? I'm sure that if I had stayed in radio or gone into landscaping with your uncle Kenny, there would have been just as many headaches."

Twenty-five years ago his father had been a late-night

disc jockey at a small radio station that played hard rock and something called New Wave. He only did it for two years, quitting to take an entry-level position in the company he was still with, but it was surprising how often he found a way to mention he had been the guy everybody knew as the Midnight Rambler. As for Uncle Kenny, he had sold his landscaping business when Sawyer was still in grade school. He lived in Hawaii now, on one of the small islands, with a house right on the beach and a boat that he took out fishing every day.

"Yeah, I'm lucky," his father said. "I love my job." He sighed a long, drawn-out sigh, topped off his coffee, and stared out the dark window to the empty backyard.

"That's why this project is perfect for you," his mother said, tapping the Career Exploration assignment sheet. The year before, the school board had voted to make it a graduation requirement, so on top of sending out college applications, doing mandatory community service and keeping up their grades, every senior in the district was writing a 3,000-word report on the job of their dreams.

"We didn't have anything like this when we were in school," his mother said, implying it was hundreds

23

and hundreds of years ago. "Back then you met with the guidance counselor once, maybe twice, and all they did was tell you to flip through a few career guides until you found something you thought you'd like. How realistic was that? I remember looking through one of those and seeing a job description for a fashion photographer and I thought, Hey, I like fashion and I like taking pictures and I have a camera—the point-and-shoot kind, not the kind you have to focus—that's what I should do. So for two months I went around taking candid pictures of my friends. I had that camera with me all the time, remember?"

"I remember," his father said without turning from the window.

"I'd get the film developed. God, that was *so* expensive. Then I'd just give them away. Crazy. My friends thought it was great—they were getting free pictures, so of course they liked it—and they all said I had a good eye, but where was I going with that?"

Sawyer shrugged. "Is that when you decided to become a receptionist?"

"Director of Initial Customer Impressions. And no, that was after college. We were married by then and you were on the way. But I was lucky because it turned out that I had a knack for the job. You know how I like to have things organized—"

"I know." Sawyer said it at the same time and in the same flat way as his father.

"—and the job is really all about organization. It comes easy for me. Like your father said, it's not always fun, but it's not awful. Besides, I have to work, so there you go. And speaking of work . . ." She tapped the assignment sheet.

"Mom, I got over a month before this is due."

As if on cue, his parents turned to look at each other, neither saying anything, keeping the obvious comments to themselves. Then his father turned back to the window and his mother turned back to him. "The first thing you have to do is pick a job," she said, reading the project requirements. "That's five points right there. What have you got so far?"

Sawyer tipped open the cover of his spiral binder and glanced inside to the blank paper. "Uh. Nothing yet."

"Nothing?" Another parent-to-parent stare.

"I'm not sure what I want to do, and I don't want to just write anything."

"Sawyer, you have forty days until this is due. That's not a lot of time."

"I remember hearing you say you wanted to be an accountant," his father said.

25

Sawyer thought about it. Math was not his subject. He was almost about average last year and hadn't made it above the curve since. It didn't come easy—if it came at all—and he couldn't see himself suddenly improving. And he couldn't remember ever saying anything about accounting. He shook his head. "I don't know, that doesn't sound like much fun."

His father laughed. "It's a job, Sawyer. It's not supposed to be fun."

"I wouldn't mind being a forensic investigator. That would be cool."

"Like on *CSI*? Please, Sawyer, be realistic. Do you have any idea how few jobs there are in that field? You have to keep *that* in mind too."

"Sometimes I build things. Out of wood and stuff. I made that shelf in the basement and I fixed my closet door. Maybe I should be a carpenter."

"No, you'd hate it," his father said. "I did it for a summer right out of high school. It was hard as hell, all day out in the sun. I hated it. No, not a carpenter."

It was quiet for a minute, then his mother said, "Well, we can't spend all night just guessing. It's going to be due before you know it and you have plenty of other things to worry about. We'll just put something down for now and you can start researching tomorrow and we can get this project done and out of the way. And if in the end it turns out it's not really the job you want to do, then you would have at least spent some time exploring it. Isn't that what this is all about, anyway?" His mother picked up a pen and flipped over the assignment sheet. Sawyer read along upside down as she wrote.

"Insurance actuary? I don't even know what that is."

"I'll tell you what that is," his father said, pointing with his coffee cup. "That's a smart call. Good money. And a lot of opportunity with health care the way it is."

"What would I do?"

"Oh, it's *very* interesting," his mother said. "There's a few in the office building where I work. They always seem happy. One of them even drives a Porsche."

His father nodded. "The Boxster? Yeah, that's sweet. You've seen it, Sawyer?"

"No. Maybe. I'm not sure. Is an actuary like an insurance agent? Because I don't think I'd—"

"You couldn't miss it," his father was saying. "Convertible. Red. Like that saltshaker."

"That's not red," his mother said. "That's more of a bright orange."

"*Orange?* No, orange is that refrigerator magnet or that bit on that magazine cover. The shaker's definitely red."

"I'm not so sure it's a convertible. Maybe it's a nine-eleven."

Sawyer rubbed the back of his neck, a headache coming on. "Dad, do you know what an insurance actuary does?"

"More or less," his father said, holding the saltshaker up against the magazine cover. "But I bet you'll be an expert by the time this project's done."

THE LAST TIME Sawyer was in this library he had been pretending to look up information on tarantulas.

He didn't need to know anything about tarantulas, their habitats, life cycles, or interactions with humans, but Dillon needed a way to accidentally run into a girl named Molly who volunteered there on the weekends. After he heard Dillon say "Hey, I didn't know you worked here," Sawyer assumed his job was done, but he hadn't planned on an overeager librarian who was absolutely thrilled to help him with his exciting research.

Thirty minutes later, Dillon had a phone number and Sawyer had a new library card, six books on arachnids, four photocopied articles, and an outline for a paper he would never write that covered tarantulas' habitats, life cycles, and interactions with humans.

That was four years ago, when Sawyer was still in eighth grade and Dillon and Garrett and Andrew were freshmen. The different-grade thing was no big deal when they were in school: a year ahead or a year behind, it was pretty much the same bullshit. Then one day they were graduates and he hadn't even started twelfth grade. Dillon left for college in August, the same weekend Garrett headed to a school in Delaware on a lacrosse scholarship. A month before that, the three of them had gone to the airport as Andrew flew off to become a Marine.

At first it was like nothing had changed. He and Dillon and Garrett would meet online most every night, teaming up to destroy hordes of radioactive mutant Nazi zombies, just like before. By October, though, Garrett was down to one night a week and Dillon started bringing on the guys in his dorm. To them, Sawyer was just another player, some guy they didn't have to bother to back up, and they sure as hell weren't going to have a *high school* student giving them orders. Mostly they ignored him. And soon, so did Dillon. He'd get a text now and then, Dillon letting him know that he wasn't going to be online that night or that he was spending the break at Sarah's parents' place or that he was sorry he missed him when he was in town last weekend. Then Dillon didn't text at all. At least not Sawyer.

Around the same time, Andrew finished basic training. He spent a week at home and they got together a couple times, but Andrew was always more of Garrett and Dillon's friend and it was weird without them around, Andrew all hardcore now, *semper fi*, gung-ho crap. When Andrew shipped out to Okinawa, Sawyer was glad to see him go.

Sawyer knew plenty of guys in his own grade, but it wasn't the same hanging out with them, and he sensed they felt the same way about him. Besides, it wasn't that bad with Zoë, and if her girlfriends were over—and they were over most of the time—that was okay too, all of them good-looking and a little wild when they got together, threatening to kick his ass in a game of strip Wii bowling or tie him up and give him a show. They never did, never even came close to doing anything like it, but there was always the chance, and a chance like that made up for a lot. Like not having any friends.

He was sitting at a table in the reference section, *The Career Finder's Almanac* propped up in front of him, trying to reread the same paragraph for the fourth time, when a rubber band arched over the top of the book and hit him on the end of his nose.

"If I was a ninja assassin, you'd be dead right now." Grace swung her backpack up on the table and sat down next to him.

"Ninja assassins don't use rubber bands to kill people."

"That's what they *want* you to think." She opened one of the reference books from his pile. "The career project? At West it's not due for another month."

"Same thing at my school," he said, guessing that since she knew the deadline she was a senior, even though she looked younger than that, especially today with that hat on. "I wanted to get it done and out of the way."

She fanned through the pages, stopping to read the captions under the pictures. "Just download something off the internet. That's what everybody else is going to do."

"Can't. My parents want to read it first and they'll know."

"Tip to the wise, Honest Abe. When downloading

papers, always add in a bunch of mistakes and typos so they have something to correct. It puts the *A* in plagiarism."

He thought about it, then thought about his parents. "They wouldn't fall for it. They want to make sure I don't screw it up and ruin my chances to get into college."

"Yeah, like it matters." She turned the pages in big hunks, back to front, front to back. "Look at this. Underwater welder. Wow, did you even know there was such a thing?" She flipped more pages. "So what do you want to be if you ever grow up?"

"*If?*"

"Just an expression."

He shrugged. "I don't know."

"No idea at all?"

"Not really, no."

"Don't you ever think about it? Dream about what it'll be like to be all on your own?"

"Of course," he said, wondering if he ever had.

"Okay. So when you're living that life, what are you doing to pay the bills?"

"A job, I guess."

"Clever. Which one?"

"I'm thinking about maybe becoming an insurance actuary."

She looked up from the book. "Yeah, right."

"Why? What's wrong with that?"

"Nothing. I just can't see you as an insurance actuary."

"Do you even know what it is?"

She was smiling, so she knew something, but she said, "No, I've got no idea. Tell me."

"They're experts in taking risks," he said, setting his book down, thumbing through the pages on his phone until he got to the notes his father had sent him. "Insurance companies use them because they don't want to pay out a lot of money. An actuary tells them the risks, that way they can charge more. A fat smoker who sits on his butt all day has to pay more for insurance than a guy who doesn't smoke and works out a lot."

"They're both gonna die. Eventually."

"Yeah, but the odds are the fat guy's gonna go first, so they charge him more."

"They need an actuary to tell them that?"

"Actuaries figure out the way to make the most money out of it."

"And if the healthy guy dies first?"

Sawyer shrugged. "I guess he wins."

"So insurance actuaries weigh fat guys for a living."

"They look at all the risks—if you drink, if you smoke, if you've got a dangerous job—"

"Like an underwater welder."

"It's all about taking risks. That's what I like about it."

She smiled again, that same knowing, smartass smile. It made her look older, and it made him uncomfortable. "What do you know about risks?"

His turn to smile. "I take my share."

"Name one."

He couldn't. Because he hadn't. At least, none that were impressive, none that were different from what any guy his age took. Drinking beer now and then, smoking pot, not that much, less than other guys, but still enough to get him in deep shit. Slipping around the parental controls on the computer and then going in to delete the search history so his mother wouldn't stumble onto the sites he'd hit. Sharing answers for the stupid fill-in-the-blank homework assignments his teachers still gave. Driving too fast. Not crazy fast, but over the speed limit. There was Zoë and the things they did, but she made sure there was no risk in that at all. And that was about it. But he couldn't tell her that, so he leaned back in the chair and drummed his fingers on the table, all casual. Let her read it any way she wanted.

"I bet you live a pretty risk-free life," she said, reading his mind.

"A couple weeks ago I helped a Swedish spy steal a treaty from the North Korean government."

"I was from Belgium."

"It was a different spy."

She laughed, and when she laughed her eyes lit up. He liked when she laughed. He raised a finger at the pile of books. "You start your career project?"

"I'm working on it right now," she said.

"Let me guess." He picked up a book and flipped the pages, stopping at random. "Elevator inspector. That's a good job for you."

"Eh, I hear it's got its ups and downs."

He flipped some more. "Protestant minister."

"I haven't got a prayer."

"Optometrist?"

She shook her head. "Can't see myself doing it. I'd like to be a surgeon but I don't think I'm cut out for it."

He laughed. It wasn't really funny but he knew he'd never think of anything that fast. He waited a few seconds, then said, "Really, what *do* you want to do?"

She tilted her head down and went back to the book.

"You've got to have some idea, I mean, if you could do anything . . ." He let it trail off and she kept turning pages like she was ignoring him. He gave her a few more seconds, then said, "Well, I guess none of us really knows what we want to do—"

"I don't care what I do," she said, "but I know how I'm going to do it. It's all part of my plan."

"Hold on. You don't have a career picked out—"

"Nope."

"But you have a plan to get it?"

"Actually it's a three-part plan, and yes, I do."

Sawyer had a career plan. He didn't know how many parts were in it. But he was sure his parents knew. "What's the first part?"

"Fun."

"Fun?"

"Yup. Whatever I end up doing, it has to be fun."

"And if it's not?"

"I won't do it. Two, I have to make a lot of money. A *real* lot."

"Everybody says that."

"But they don't get it. I will."

"Because it's part of your plan."

"Exactly."

"And the third part?"

"That's the most important one. I'm going to be a celebrity."

The way she said it, quick, like she was throwing it at him, past him, without looking up and with no laugh in her voice, he knew she meant it, but without thinking, reflex taking over, he said, "That's impossible." He heard himself say it and tried to pull it back, but it was too late, it was out there and he sensed something, a ripple maybe, and then it was gone and she was staring at him, smiling.

"My first choice was to be an insurance actuary," she said, and the light was back in her eyes, "but *everybody* wants to do that these days. So I'll settle for being a celebrity."

She was good-looking, but not stunning, not like Zoë with her long blond hair and lineless tan. And she didn't have the body Zoë had either—Grace was short, small boobs like a gymnast. They had different smiles, too. Zoë's was better, like a toothpaste ad, and when Grace smiled the corners of her mouth twisted a bit. And Grace had those weird eyes. So yeah, good-looking, but still not stunning, not like Zoë, not like a model. Or a celebrity.

"Can you sing?"

She laughed loud enough to get a *shhhh* from an old man at the magazine rack. "What, I can't get by on my looks?"

"I never said—"

"Relax. I'm not stupid. I know what I look like. Cute, sure, but not hot. That girl there, the one coming in? *That's* hot."

Sawyer looked across the library and watched as Zoë took off her hat, shook her head, and ran a hand through her hair.

"That's my girlfriend," he said.

"*Really?* Hey, not bad for an insurance actuary." She slipped out of the chair and picked up her backpack, slinging it over her shoulder. "See you around," she said, tapping a finger along the side of her nose.

He took a quick glance over at Zoë, checking her phone for messages.

"Wait, where's that from again?" he asked.

"What? This?"

"Yeah, that nose thing. Where's it from?"

Another glance. A few seconds, tops.

"Hope you've got a good memory," Grace said, and then rattled off seven numbers before heading down an aisle of reference books and disappearing into the stacks.

CHAPTER

6

"THERE," ZOË SAID, brushing the hair out of her face as she sat up on the couch. "Don't ever say we never do it."

Sawyer wanted to say that he never said that, but he knew that he did, that he said it so often she probably didn't hear him when he said it. Maybe that was why they never did it. Instead he said nothing, leaning back on the warm pillows, trying not to sweat all over her shirt.

They had only been dating a month when her parents sat them both down and gave them the Talk, reminding Zoë that she had taken a purity pledge at church and letting Sawyer know that they expected him to be a gen-. tleman and see that she honored that pledge.

It was a good talk, just three weeks too late.

But even before that first time, Sawyer could sense the way it was going to be, because as much as she talked about it, as much as she liked to play the naughty-girl role in front of her friends, she found actually doing it kinda gross. And when they fooled around, which wasn't happening all that much anymore, he could forget about even suggesting the things that she told her friends she loved to do.

Well, if he didn't like it, he could always try to find another girlfriend. But if he did, Zoë would be pissed and she had a wicked temper and her girlfriends would all turn against him, so maybe he wouldn't find another girlfriend. His mom would be pissed too. No, not pissed. *Disappointed*. She liked Zoë, and when Zoë came over, they would spend hours watching cooking shows or vampire romance movies. Sawyer had the feeling that his mom knew that they had done it and that meant that she'd expect him to do the right thing, even if he didn't know what that was.

This wasn't the way he wanted it to be, but it could have been worse, and it could still change, and besides, it was better than no sex at all.

"What time is it?"

Sawyer reached down to his ankles and got his phone

out of his pocket. "Three forty-eight."

Zoë picked his T-shirt off the floor and tossed it on his chest. "My parents are going to be home in two hours, and I've got a lot to get done. I've gotta shower and do my hair again, thank you very much."

"Anytime. I'm ready."

"Ugh, please. It hasn't even been two minutes."

He sat up, put on his shirt, and pulled up his jeans. He still had his sneakers on, another one of Zoë's rules.

"Then I think I'll make cookies. If I light candles again, my parents will start with the questions." Her elbow was on the arm of the couch, her chin in her palm, and she looked at him, her lips tight together. She watched as, still sitting, he zippered his fly and pushed his phone back in his front pocket, then she said, "You wear too much cologne. How do you put it on?"

"It's body spray. I spray it on my body."

"No. What you're supposed to do is spritz some in the air and walk through it." She used her free hand to illustrate the spritzing, then a little wave to show him where to walk. "My parents can always tell when you've been here. Now I have to make cookies."

Sawyer stretched, working the knot out of his back from the weird angle he had been lying in. Zoë made excellent cookies, usually from scratch, though she'd use a mix this time, done in twenty minutes. But any kind of cookie sounded about perfect right then.

"You don't need a ride back to the library, do you? Cuz I've got a lot to do."

He sighed. "I guess I can walk."

"Don't get whiney. It's not far. What, maybe a half mile?"

"It's more than that."

She shook her head. "No, it's not. I used to walk there all the time when I was a kid. It's not even a half mile."

He had left his car at the library. It would have made sense for him to drive it to her house, but that would have meant that it would have been in the driveway the whole time, right where the neighbors could see it, and there was no way she could let that happen. So he drove with her, scooching down in the passenger seat of her car as she pulled into the garage, and now he'd have to walk back to the library, which was closer to three miles, a distance Sawyer knew that Zoë had never walked.

"What were you doing there, anyway?" she said.

"That career project. I told you when you called."

"Why? It's not due for weeks. You should be worried

about precalculus, not that stupid thing." She stood, hitched up her jeans, and snaked her belt back through the loops. "You think anybody's ever going to read those? They're not even graded. I'm just going to download mine. Everybody's doing it that way."

"That's what I hear." He watched her gather up the pillows from the floor and from the recliner, fluffing each one before placing them back on the couch. Overhead, cold autumn rain pelted the skylight. "What do you want to be if you ever grow up?"

"You mean what am I going to download? I don't know. I'll ask your mom. She'll know."

"Why don't you ask Linda?"

"Because Linda is an idiot. She'd just tell me to *follow my bliss* and *find my own road*."

Linda liked it when Zoë's friends called her Linda and not Mrs. Whittaker, or worse, Zoë's mom. Sawyer was never comfortable with it, and when he was around Zoë's mother he avoided calling her anything at all.

"She's not like *your* mom," Zoë said. "Your mom is cool. She does all that school stuff for you and doesn't bitch about it. She got you that job—"

"My father got me the job."

"Same thing. And she doesn't freak out if you swear in front of her. Seriously, Sawyer, you've got no idea how lucky you are."

She was right about the job, it was the same thing, but she was wrong about the swearing, at least when *he* swore. And he should've known how lucky he was. His mother said it enough.

"What did your mom say you should be?"

"An insurance actuary."

She stopped mid-fluff and looked at him. "See what I mean? That's perfect."

"Perfect? Do you know what they do?"

"Who cares? All you need to do is pick a job that sounds serious. You put down stunt driver or porn star, you know they're gonna read it. I bet no one else is going to turn in a report on an insurance actually."

"Actuary."

"Whatever. No one else is going to pick it."

"There's a reason for that."

"You can download the whole thing. You won't even have to change a word." She laughed, amazed. "Your mom's a genius."

He started to say something, then jumped off the

couch when the screen door rattled, the wind whipping across the porch like an angry father ready to walk in on them.

"Holy shit, that scared the crap out of me." Zoë held her hand to her chest and moved to the window, peeking between the slats of the blinds. "If that had been my parents . . . oh my god."

The wind howled and the door rattled again, but this time they didn't jump.

"It's really getting bad out there," she said, turning away from the windows. "You'd better get going."

His parents were out when he got home—some after-work function at his father's office—so he took a hot shower to warm up. It was his first night home alone in weeks, so he nuked a mini frozen pizza, poured his Belgian golden ale into a tall glass, and spent a quality evening watching *Jackass* online.

CHAPTER

7

IT TOOK HIM longer to find the apartment than he thought it would. He knew the road it was on, a divided highway on the west side, but it was tucked around behind a strip mall, and the entrance, unmarked, was squeezed between a Burger King and an auto-parts store that had gone out of business before Sawyer started high school. He was driving past it for the fifth time when he spotted the green mailbox she had told him to look for.

Six cars in the parking lot—two minivans, two pickups, a junker on cinder blocks, and a Corvette. It was the middle of the afternoon, so either the residents were all at work or there weren't that many residents to begin with.

There were eight buildings in the complex, each with four apartments—two up, two down—and a laundry room on the lower level. The buildings were identical once but different now, some missing their fake shutters, some with the plastic brick façade peeling away from the plywood. It wasn't ghetto, wasn't even trailer park, but it was heading that way.

The door to the building was propped open with a hunk of concrete that had once been part of the walkway. He went up to the landing and knocked. He could hear her inside, and for a second, maybe longer, he imagined her opening the door wearing just a towel, a small one, barefoot, her hair still wet from the shower. But as the security chain came off and the bolt clicked and the door opened, he knew it wouldn't be like that.

"I was hoping it was you," Grace said, stepping back to give him room to come in. "For some reason they put the peephole six feet up. I didn't want to have to drag a chair all the way from the kitchen to look out."

"You should've checked. I could have been a bad guy."

She grinned and brought a foot-long kitchen knife from behind her back.

"Whoa. Good thing you recognized me."

"Yeah," she said, moving over to a desk, dropping the knife into an open drawer, then bumping the drawer closed with her hip. "Wouldn't want to make that mistake again."

He had assumed the inside of the apartment would match the building, but he was wrong. It was straight off one of those home-makeover shows Zoë watched, with light gray walls, bright white trim, spotless white leather furniture, matching bookcases lined with picture frames and thick glass bowls filled with clear glass marbles, a weird painting hanging by the balcony. Down the hallway was the kitchen and across from that, the bathroom, then a closed door that was probably a bedroom. Everything in the apartment was modern and expensive. At least, it looked expensive. But what was the deal with the TV?

"My aunt's even shorter than me," Grace said, holding her hand out shoulder high as they both looked over at the thirty-odd-inch flat-screen, mounted on the wall about a foot off the new gray carpet, the top of the monitor not quite at Sawyer's waist. "All day long she has to look up at people. When she comes home, she likes to look down on them. And it doesn't hurt your neck, especially when you sit on the floor."

He took it as a cue and sat down, leaning against the bottom of the couch, eye-level with the screen. "What do you want to drink?" Grace said as she walked to the kitchen.

He heard the fridge open. "Any beer?"

"Of course. But we're not having any."

"You don't like beer?"

"I love beer. But we're not having any here."

"Would your aunt know?"

"Probably not, but I would. That's why she lets me hang out here when she's at work. I gave her my word I'd be good."

"And no drinking was one of her rules?"

"There weren't any rules, she just told me to be good."

"And you gave your word."

"My word's all I got. And some diet cream soda."

He listened as she dropped ice cubes into tall glasses. "I didn't think you'd call," she said.

He wasn't going to. When she gave him her phone number at the library, he didn't bother to write it down. If Zoë saw a strange number on a page in his notebook or on his phone, she'd have questions and he'd have lies, but she'd call the number anyway—*Who's this? Why you giving my boyfriend your skank number?*—playing the role because that's what you did when you found a strange number where there shouldn't be a strange number. It'd be a lot of hassle for nothing. So he didn't even try to remember it. But two days later, for no reason he could figure, the number was still there, right in the front of his mind. And that was the reason he dialed the number from the phone in the back room of Mike's Ice Cream.

"When I saw your girlfriend come in, I said to myself, There's no way he's calling you."

"Yeah, she's really hot," he said, knowing it sounded wrong as the words were coming out, but if it bothered her, she didn't let it show.

"That's not why." She sat down next to him, not close but close enough to hand him his drink. "I could tell by looking at her, she's got you by the short hairs. You ain't going nowhere."

"It's *not* like that."

It *was* like that and he knew it, but he hadn't heard it since Dillon had left for college, and he didn't expect it from her.

"I'm not saying she's not nice, I'm just saying she's

the type who likes to be in charge. Nothing wrong with that." She messed with the remote. "I mean, if that's what you're into."

"I'm here, ain't I?"

"Calm down, tiger. I'm just yanking your chain. I'm glad you called." She looked over at him and smiled. It was a real smile, nothing hidden behind it.

"So what's this movie that I *ab*-solutely, *pos*-itively must, *must*, MUST have to see?"

"It's *The Sting*, from 1973, directed by George Roy Hill, starring Paul Newman and Robert Redford, a hundred and twenty-nine minutes, four and a half stars, and if you make fun of me one more time, you're out. Now, you ready for this?"

The movie didn't suck as bad as he thought it would, a couple of con men back in the 1930s ripping off a rich gangster with an elaborate plan that would have probably made sense if she weren't talking through the whole thing. She loved the two main actors, hated the music, thought the hats were great, liked the old guy, didn't trust the waitress, swore that she saw the one gangster in another movie, and jumped when the gun went off, even though she'd seen the movie a dozen times before. She paused it at the end, freezing a shot of the Johnny Hooker character tapping the side of his nose.

"That's a classic signal right there," she said, acting it out in case he had missed it. "You see that, you know the fix is in."

"So is that how you're going to become a celebrity? Pull an elaborate con game on a mob boss?"

She glared at him, then laughed. "It's not nice to make fun of a girl and her dreams."

"You're only kidding about that, right? You don't really want to be a celebrity, do you?"

"Why not?"

"It's not realistic, that's why."

"Oh, and being an actuary for an insurance company *is* realistic?"

"You can go to school to be an insurance actuary—"

"No, *you* can go to school for it."

"—but you can't just decide to become a celebrity. That's not how it works. You have to be famous for something."

"Give me time."

"And you just can't start at the top."

"Watch me," Grace said. "It's go big or go home."

"Besides, what's so great about being a celebrity?"

Bang. She sat up at that. "Oh my god, *everything*! Check it out. You get into all the clubs, people give you hot clothes and jewelry for no reason, you've got photographers everywhere you go, you're on TV *all* the time, *millions* of people follow you online, and if you're *really* famous, if you're a *true* celebrity, then you get your own reality show."

He looked at her, the way she was beaming, her eyes all lit up, her smile somehow brighter. He shrugged. "You didn't seem like the reality-TV type."

"Yeah, well you don't seem like the insurance type either."

"Those shows are so stupid—"

"Don't be judging just because people like stuff you don't like. I think they're fun."

"And you want to be on one."

"Yup."

He thought of something and grinned. "Well, there *are* ways to get on those shows, you know. Like that one girl, the fake Italian . . ."

"The one that screws everybody in sight?" She waved him off. "No way."

"It worked for her."

"Yeah, well if that's all it took, three-quarters of the

girls at my school would be megastars. No, I'm going to be a celebrity, and I'm going to have my own show, and I'm going to do it my way. You'll see."

She hit the Play button, and the credits rolled while he thought about the girls at West High.

THIS IS THE joke Sawyer's precalculus teacher told the first day of school: A teacher's standing in front of the class, explaining a precalc equation, and there's this big football player, we'll call him Billy, sitting in the last row, and he's completely lost. The teacher's talking and Billy keeps sighing and yawning, not really disrupting the class, but making his presence known. Finally Billy raises his hand. Hey teach, I got a question. Yes, Billy? Why do we need to take this class? The teacher looks straight at him and says, Because calculus saves lives. Billy scratches his head and thinks about if for a second, then says, Hey teach, how does calculus save lives? And the teacher says, It keeps guys like you out of medical school.

Not funny, but Sawyer got it.

It was one of the last things he got in that class.

Not that he hadn't been trying. He assumed he had to have a good grade in the class since that's what his guidance counselor kept telling him, but then his father didn't seem all that worried that he was failing, hinting that there were "things in the works" and "irons in the fire," whatever that meant. His mother offered to help. She'd aced precalc in high school. Hadn't used it since, not even in college, but hey, it was like falling off a bike, right?

Right. That feeling of being out of control, of falling— no, of crashing, not able to do anything about it, that panic just before hitting the pavement, skin scraping off, bones buckling under the pressure, feeling it all before it happened, the scars that took forever to heal, and that sour feeling in the pit of your stomach the next time you tried it? Yeah, that was precalc.

But that wasn't the worst feeling. He'd get through the class—eventually—not with the best grade but with a passing one, and he'd get his diploma and he'd go off to college. Precalculus would go away. But there was another feeling, one he couldn't nail down, one that came late at night or when he went for a run or when it was slow at Mike's Ice Cream or like now, in precalc, Mr. Young up there speaking in tongues, *that* feeling—he wondered if it would be with him for the rest of his life.

It wasn't lost.

Lost was what you felt when you didn't know where to go or how to get there. All you needed were directions and you wouldn't be lost. He knew where he had to go and what he had to do to get there, the directions clearer than the ones that came with his phone. Get good grades, get into college, get more good grades, get a career, get money, get married, get kids, get old, get on with it. So it wasn't lost.

Was it drifting, was that the feeling? That sense that he was simply floating along without a plan, wondering where he'd land when he washed up on shore? No, that wasn't it, he had had a perfect plan handed to him, and the plan told him exactly where he'd land. It couldn't have been drifting. Drifting actually sounded pretty good.

Besides, he was going too fast to be drifting.

Here's what he knew—he had a direction and he had a plan. They weren't his, but they seemed to be working.

And he had a hot girlfriend and a car of his own and an okay job and a future as an insurance actuary. What was he complaining about? He had it good. He knew all that.

But it didn't make that feeling go away.

Grace was the one with no plan. Celebrity? Come on, what was she thinking? That's the kind of dream you have when you're ten, like him thinking he'd grow up to be Batman. It was stupid to hold on to dreams like that. Maybe that's why he liked hanging around her. Next to her, he looked smart. At least career-wise.

But there was something about her, something different. She was cute, yeah, and she'd pop into his head now and then, but so did any halfway-decent-looking girl, not much control there. It wasn't like he was going to hit on her. She didn't seem like the type anyway, probably a virgin but you never know, and besides, he had Zoë. The movie was okay, sorta, but watching it with her was fun. There's a lot more movies you *have* to see, she had said, and he groaned when she pulled a list out of her pocket, but really it was good because he'd get to watch them with her, and then he was back to wondering what it was about her he liked in the first place.

Then the bell rang and Mr. Young said what he always said at the end of every class: "I hope you learned something today."

Sawyer had learned something that day.

He learned he'd never get into medical school.

"ONE GUY, EIGHT hot girls. It's like the plot of *every* porno out there."

That was Zoë's girlfriend Renée and that's how Renée liked to talk, the clique's self-appointed expert on all things X-rated.

She was right about the numbers. There were seven girls in the oversized rec room at Zoë's house, and there was one guy, Sawyer, and the girls were hot, no doubt about it, in their tight jeans and short shorts, even the two in baggy sweat pants—waistbands below their hips, baby-doll T-shirts under their unzipped hoodies—even they were hot. But she was wrong about it being like every porno out there.

First off, it wasn't always one guy and seven girls.

Sawyer had seen enough pornos online—bits of them, anyway—to know Renée didn't know what she was talking about.

As usual.

Second, one guy and seven girls wasn't a plot, it was a cast. It might make the plot more interesting, but it wasn't a plot. Anyway, from what he'd seen, pornos didn't need plots.

Third—and this was the one that bugged him the most—girls in pornos didn't spend the whole night wolfing down bags of sour cream and onion potato chips and stacks of chocolate-covered Double Stuf Oreos, chugging Diet Cokes to win burping contests while they texted their boyfriends, texted girls who weren't there, and texted the boyfriends of the girls they were sitting right next to. Add in the direct-to-video chick flicks on the HDTV, the just-shoot-me dance music on the stereo, and a parent peeking in the door every five minutes to make sure there wasn't any alcohol, and you had a typical Friday night at Zoë's. So even if it were the plot of *every* porno out there, it wasn't going anywhere.

Sawyer racked up the balls for another game of pool. He played by himself, eight ball, switching from stripes to solids and back again with every missed shot. He switched a lot. Tatiana was good at pool, and if she were there he'd challenge her to a game. She'd beat him, sure, she beat him every time they played, but that was okay. She'd been playing her whole life and nobody beat her. Tatiana had a boyfriend now, one who didn't like spending his Friday nights at Zoë's house, so Sawyer played alone. He could have asked Taylor or Meagan or Sandra or Lori or any of the others, but they were worse than he was and lost interest after their first missed shot, which was early in the game. Besides, they didn't have time for games, not with all that serious texting to be done.

He lined up the cue ball, drew back, and broke. The balls scattered but nothing dropped.

On the couch, Meagan was digging the last of the caramel corn out of the bag, asking anyone who was listening if they had heard back from any colleges yet. Jessica laughed.

"It's not even Thanksgiving. I'm still working on the applications."

"Just wondering. I sent mine out last week and I was hoping that—"

"What? You think you're going to hear back *already*? Don't be stupid."

"Ms. Brody says you won't hear until February, after

they've checked your financial-aid forms."

"Yeah, right. Like I'm gonna get financial aid."

"I got accepted already," Zoë said without looking up from her phone, owning the moment.

Sawyer stopped mid-backstroke, listening in to the news.

"You *did*? Where?"

"Wembly."

There was a pause. "Oh."

"What do you mean, '*Oh*'?"

Meagan shrugged. "I thought you were going away to school."

"Changed my mind. I met some of the girls from Kappa Kappa Gamma. They told me I'd have no problem getting in."

"To *Wembly*?"

"Duh. To KKG. I got in to Wembly no problem."

Sandra said, "I heard that they don't even look at you if you don't get a two thousand on your SATs."

"That's a lie," Renée said, and immediately they all assumed it was true. But then if Zoë *did* get in . . .

"KKG is great," Lori said, "but isn't Wembly a bit, I don't know, *conservative* for you?"

"What's that supposed to mean?"

"No coed dorms, visiting hours, guests gotta sign in at the desk or get buzzed in, guys can't sleep over. And they've got all those rules about smoking and drinking . . ."

"So? What's your point?"

"It sounds kinda like what you have now."

"You make it sound like a prison. Besides, that's only when you're a freshman and you have to live in the dorms. Sophomore year I'll move into KKG. That'll be insane."

From the beanbag chair, Taylor said, "My parents want me to go to a state school."

"Go. It'd be better than staying here."

"Nothing wrong with staying here," Zoë said.

"Not if you're *Kappa Kappa Gamma*."

Sawyer blinked, then shifted his weight before realigning his shot, still thinking about what Zoë said. And how every school he was applying to was at least two hours away.

"What are you smiling about," Lori said, giving Sawyer a little hip-check as she walked past on her way to the bathroom. He laughed, then shot without looking, nailing the seven ball into the far corner pocket.

Andrea said, "I know this guy, Tyree, he goes to West. He just found out he got a full-ride scholarship to State."

"What do you expect?" Meagan said. "West's got the best basketball team in the county."

"Not because of Tyree. He's pure geek. They say he's a genius."

"And he goes to *West*? Don't believe it."

"I have a few friends at West," Sandra said, ripping open a fresh bag of Cheez Doodles. "I think they're pretty smart."

"Said the girl who's not taking any AP classes."

"That's because of band. You know my schedule's all screwed up. Don't be such a little bitch."

"Well, I wouldn't have to be if you weren't—"

"This girl came into Mike's the other day, looking for a job," Sawyer said, talking loud enough to drown out Zoë, making it up as he went. "She goes to West. Her application said she was on the high honor roll."

"At West that's a C-minus," Renée said.

"She had a weird name. Grace something. Know her?"

"Nope. But I'll ask my friend Lindsey," Sandra said, her thumbs jumping around the keypad. "She knows everyone there."

Zoë laughed. "There's something to be proud of."

It took two more games of solo pool and another

67

twenty minutes of painful movie before Sandra got her answer.

"That girl? Grace? She's a nobody. Lindsey says she a loser."

Sawyer stepped away from his shot and chalked up the cue. "Could be more than one Grace at West."

"No, Lindsey says she's the only one," Sandra said, texting as she read the screen. "Was she short?"

"I guess, yeah."

"Wore a stupid hat?"

"Maybe. I don't remember," he said, remembering the hat she wore to the library, the one that didn't look stupid at all, the one that looked a lot cooler than Andrea's ridiculous pink hair or Jessica's eyebrow ring.

"She's a loser. She's got abso-zero friends. Even the foreign-exchange students avoid her."

He squinted down the cue. "She didn't seem that weird."

"Trust me, she is. Lindsey knows everybody at West and if she says somebody's a loser, they're a loser. Don't let her get hired, you might have to work with her."

Bang. The four ball rattled in the pocket. "That doesn't seem fair."

Sandra laughed. "So? What do *you* care?"

"Yeah," Zoë said, looking over from her seat on the couch, head down just a bit so her eyes were glaring out from under her arched brows. "What do *you* care?"

"I don't," Sawyer said, hitting the cue ball low and hard, launching it off the table and across the hardwood floor.

CHAPTER

10

SUNDAYS WERE THE busiest days at Mike's Ice Cream. In the summer the line would stretch across the room, sometimes out the door. There'd be three people behind the counter and one working the register, everybody busting their ass to keep ahead of the rush. It was crazy but it was better that way. The time flew by and the tip jar would be heavy with change, maybe some bills, the tips split evenly, everybody getting a few bucks extra for doing the work they had to do anyway.

That all changed when the weather turned cold. The lines were gone and the hours dragged by and there wasn't enough to do to keep one person busy, let alone the two that Mike left on the Sunday schedule. The college students that had been home for the summer were long gone by then, so were most of the owner's relatives who helped out on the weekends. All that was left were high school kids and a few retirees who were just tickled to death to have something productive to do to with their time. And as he watched them mop the mud off the floor or refill the rainbow sprinkles bin, Sawyer had to wonder what they considered an unproductive use of their time.

Francis McGillicutty used to be the regional sales manager for a company that did something with hydraulic systems for tractors and forklifts. Now he made the best darn banana splits this side of the Mississippi, and he'd tell you that every time he made one.

"The secret is in how you chop up the nuts," he said as he squirted chocolate sauce over the fat scoops of chocolate, vanilla, and strawberry ice cream.

Sawyer, so mindlessly bored that he watched Francis work, said, "We're not supposed to use a knife."

"I chopped these up last night. Got to thinking about our shift and the customers that would be coming in, and what they'd want. Something told me I'd be making a few of these today, so I picked up a can of Spanish peanuts and got them ready. Good thing I did, too."

Sawyer hadn't thought about his shift until he pulled up in the parking lot, and he couldn't remember ever thinking about what the customers might want before they asked for it. All the old employees were like that, always *going that extra mile* and *giving 110 percent*, making everyone else look like a slacker. It was easy for them—they didn't have lives.

Francis handed his masterpiece to the only customer they had seen since noon, a guy who definitely didn't need another ice cream, then he took forever to work the touch-screen cash register and give the guy his change.

The customer left, wolfing it down, and Francis watched him go, smiling the whole time.

"I think that's just about my favorite part of the job."

"Yeah, not getting a tip is my favorite, too."

"You've got to take pride in your work. I made that fella the best banana split he's ever going to eat. That's a good feeling. See, I look at it like this. You've got to find out what it is you like to do, then—"

"I know, I know. You'll never work a day in your life. I've heard it a few times before."

Francis nodded. "Good for you, but that's not what I was going to say. What I was going to say—before you interrupted—is that you've got to find out what it is you like to do, then go and do it."

"Sounds like the same thing to me."

"Not if you think about it. According to you, if I find something I like to do and I do it, it won't be work."

"It's just this thing my father says, I really don't—"

"No offense, but just because your pop says it, that doesn't make it accurate. See, I like making sundaes and I make a mean banana split, but at the end of the day it's still a job. And the day they stop paying me is the day I stop coming in. What *I* said was that once you find out what it is you like to do, you have to go do it."

"Oh, I get it now, thanks," Sawyer said, checking the time on the digital clock behind the counter. Three hours, forty-seven minutes to go.

"No, you don't. You're just saying that to shut me up. But that's okay, you're young, you'll see for yourself soon enough." He laughed as he said it, so Sawyer laughed too, embarrassed that he was that easy to see through.

"You think I wanted to be a regional salesman my whole life? *Hell* no. Who wants to do that? I wanted to be a crop-dusting pilot. Up there in the clouds, buzzing low over the fields, doing loop-dee-loops, taking the girls for a ride. But did I go do it? No, I did not. I knew what I wanted to do and instead did what everybody else wanted me to do. Now don't get me wrong, I've had a good life—married fifty-six years, four lovely daughters, a bunch of grandkids, a nice home, all paid for, promotions at my job, won a few sales awards, new car every five years—"

"Making banana splits," Sawyer said, joking around, but Francis didn't seem to hear him.

"Yup, it's been a good life. Just not the one I wanted. And now it's all but done."

Sawyer swept some crumbs off the counter with his hand, then wiped his hand on his apron. What are you supposed to say to that? *Sorry your life sucked? Sorry you never lived your dream? Sorry you're going to be dead soon?* Great, now only three hours, forty-*six* minutes to go.

"So, Sawyer, what is it *you* want to do?"

A long pause, then a quick "I don't know," his hand sweeping across the empty counter, insurance actuary not even in the back of his mind.

"Better think of something, and soon," Francis said as they both watched a young couple negotiate a stroller through the front door, a cold breeze slipping in with them. "If you don't know what you want, you can't complain about what you get."

CHAPTER
11

"**ON MY EIGHTEENTH** birthday, my dad bought me my first legal beer," Sawyer's father said as he handed his son the frosty mug. "Too bad you gotta be twenty-one now."

Sawyer turned the mug so that the straw slid around, then sipped his Olde Tyme Root Beer, his back teeth tingling, either from the cold or the sugar.

His mother said, "Cheers," and they all clinked glasses over the basket of complimentary nachos. It was a Wednesday, a lousy day for a birthday, but it wasn't like he could do anything different on this one that he couldn't have on the last one or on the next. His birthday wouldn't matter again for three more years, and his birthday wish

for this year was that he wouldn't be spending that one with his parents in a booth at Applebee's.

"I can't believe my little boy is eighteen," his mother said for the fifth time since they had left the house, Sawyer driving the five miles in his father's Explorer, his dad telling him the whole way to watch the road and leave the radio alone. "It seems like just yesterday that I rocked him to sleep."

"It *was* yesterday," his father said, laughing at his attempt at a joke, Sawyer and his mother acting like they didn't hear it.

There were a lot of restaurants in town, but his parents stuck to the chains. Applebee's, Chili's, Olive Garden, T.G.I. Friday's, Outback, Red Lobster—those down-home, family-friendly, corporate kinds of places. They each had their own unique look, but inside their two-foot-tall menus it was all the same stuff. One place's Chicken Tenders was another's Chicken Crisps, the Quesadilla Burger here was the Big Mex there, and no matter what they called it, the special sauce wasn't all that special. Sawyer had grown up eating in one chain or another, the big night out, complete with dessert. He used to love it. The kid's menu, the balloons, the free

refills, the place mats you could draw on. But then it was easy to impress an eight-year-old. Now? They were okay, he guessed. He had the menus memorized and there were never any surprises. And his parents were paying. If it were up to him, they'd be at the New Fong Chinese Quick Takeout, waiting on a double order of kung pao chicken and fried rice.

But it was never up to him, so they went to the chains.

Sawyer was trying to remember if he liked the Applebee's version of the Mushroom-Swiss Burger he had at Friday's when he felt the hostess's upper thigh humping against his arm.

"You ready to order?" Zoë said, somehow making the red polo and black pants uniform look sexy. She worked part time as a hostess, claiming she had to save for college but knowing that her parents would pay for everything. Her parents joked that the only reason she got the job was so that she could tell customers where to sit and busboys what to clean. Sawyer didn't like it when she played waitress, partly because she was too busy to talk, partly because she always got his order wrong. But it was his birthday and his parents wanted to take him out and he wanted to see Zoë, so he guessed it was all right.

His father said, "Are there any specials on the menu today?" and the way he said it, his voice all game-show host, Sawyer knew something was up. It was too early for the stupid birthday song, the one where the whole waitstaff comes marching over, clapping and singing, making everybody in the place look at the birthday boy. That would come later, he could bet on it.

"*Wellll . . . ,*" Zoë said. That proved it, something was up. She opened the menu she was carrying and took out a white envelope. "Today we have something *really* special."

She handed the envelope to Sawyer. It was addressed to him, with the blue and yellow Wembly College logo on the front. And it was already ripped open.

"Go ahead, read it," his mom said, as if he didn't know what to do.

Zoë slid in next to him as he took out the letter and started reading.

"Congratulations, your application for early admission has been accepted. On behalf of the entire Wembly College community—"

"I'm *so* proud of you, son."

"I knew he could do it," his father said, slipping the letter from Sawyer's fingers, folding it back into the envelope. "He's always been smart."

Zoë put her arms around his neck and pulled him in for a fast in-front-of-the-parents kiss, then gave him a hug and whispered things in his ear his parents would never believe.

His mother reached across the table and patted the back of his hand. "How's *that* for a birthday surprise?"

Well, it pretty much sucked.

He had heard about Wembly since he was a kid, how his parents went there, how it was once ranked one of the top 500 small-to-medium-size private liberal-arts colleges, how the men's swim team placed third in its division sometime last century, how it had a really good reference library. But what he remembered most was that it was eighteen miles from his house—less than a half-hour commute, even in bad weather—and that if he went there, he could stay in town and live at home. And with Zoë going there, it'd be just like high school all over again. He had assumed that his low grade in precalc, while good enough to get him into other schools, would be too far below Wembly's legendary high standards. Apparently those standards weren't that high after all.

So, yeah, it sucked.

But Sawyer knew this wasn't the time to bring it up.

He wasn't sure when that time would come, but as he looked at the envelope in his father's hands, he knew he'd have to start figuring that out soon.

"Aw, look. He's so surprised he's speechless," Zoë said, pinching his cheek.

"Gosh," he said, "I don't even remember finishing the application."

His parents smiled at each other and Sawyer knew right then what had happened.

"It was on your list of schools," his father said, "and we understand you have a lot on your plate right now."

"Turns out your father golfs with somebody in the admissions department—"

"Not *somebody*. The dean of admissions."

"—and he said that he can authorize early admissions, especially for legacy applicants."

"Liz and I both went to Wembly," his father explained to Zoë, who had heard it a hundred times before.

Sawyer kept smiling as he took a breath. "This is great, really." Pause. Keep smiling. Give them the moment but plant the seed. "There's a few schools I still want to send applications to, but this is great."

"You're not going to find a better school. You know

how much your father and I loved going there."

"It's a *great* school. That's why I picked it," Zoë said, forgetting to mention that whole Kappa Kappa Gamma thing.

"Yeah, it is a good school, but there's a couple others I like, and I think maybe I can get a scholarship."

"It's a nice idea, son," his father said. "But for the money you'd get, *if* you got anything . . ."

"We've been saving for you to go to college since before you were born, so it's not really the money."

His father nodded, picking up the menu. "Plus you'd be commuting anyway. That's a big savings right there. Better than a scholarship. And you don't have to leave home to get it."

"I'll be living on campus, but we'll probably see each other even more. I mean, it's not like you can *stay* there overnight or anything, but they have an *amazing* common area where we can hang out," Zoë said, and she kept a straight face as she said it, the others going along with the ridiculous story.

"And as far as that precalc class goes, I told Gary all about it. You've already earned enough math credits to graduate, that's just something extra. He says you should drop it, focus on your other classes. Bet you're glad to hear that."

"Sure. But like I was saying, if I get a good grade in precalc, I can still get—"

"Your future's all set, son. Only one decision you have to worry about," his father said from behind his menu. "What to order for dinner."

CHAPTER

12

SHE NARROWED HER eyes and tried to look tough. "That was an American cinema masterpiece," she said, the corners of her mouth twitching up into a smile. "What do you mean it was *'okay'*?"

"Okay's good," he said, then laughed as he dodged the pillow that came flying off the couch.

"You're talking about the Marx Brothers. I'll accept brilliant, hilarious, or comedic perfection. *Good* doesn't even come close."

When Grace had texted that she'd downloaded *Animal Crackers*, Sawyer did what he'd done for the other films they had watched since *The Sting*—he checked the online reviews, reading enough to know what he was in for. This one was yet another black-and-white movie from a thousand years ago, and the plot—what there was of one—had something to do with a stolen painting.

"There were parts that were really funny," Sawyer said. "That scene with the card game, that was good."

"You mean great?"

"I mean good. Now when they stole that guy's birth-mark? *That* was great."

"What about Groucho?"

"Very cool. I liked how he didn't care what people thought about him, he just did whatever he wanted."

"My hero," she said, batting her eyes and pretending to swoon.

Sawyer ran a finger along his upper lip. "I'm going to grow a mustache like his."

"It was painted on."

"Fine. I'm going to paint on a mustache like his."

"What'd you think of Harpo? And careful, he's my favorite."

"He was my favorite too. Until he played the harp. That was torture."

"True. But I fast-forwarded through it."

"Not fast enough."

She leaned back against the couch, their shoulders

almost touching. "So what did you like best?"

That's easy. It was her. How she talked through the whole thing, repeating the lines she swore were hilarious and explaining the jokes that she thought he didn't get. They still weren't funny, but the way she explained them—all excited, her voice changing for each character, jumping up to act out the scenes—now *that* was funny. But she didn't need to be told any of that. The way he had been laughing, she knew.

Part of it was just watching movies together. They were good, not all of them, sure, but most of them, and some of them he liked a lot, the ones with Humphrey Bogart and Lauren Bacall and Robert Mitchum and Marilyn Monroe. Especially the ones with Marilyn Monroe. And he liked talking about the movies too—*really* talking—about stuff like characters and symbolism and camera angles and other things he'd never noticed before but thought about now that she pointed them out, things that made even the old movies better, things he knew Zoë would find boring.

If it didn't sound so lame, he would've told Grace the real truth. The best part was hanging out with her. She was easy to talk to and he could be himself. Well, as much of himself as he could be with somebody else. She never told him what to do or what to think, listening as he rambled on about some part of a movie he liked, looking at him as he spoke, waiting until he got the idea out as good as it was going to get before jumping in, letting him know when she thought he was right and calling him out on the bullshit. Just like he could do with her. So yeah, hanging out together, that was the best part, like it used to be when he hung out with Dillon and Garrett and Andrew. But he was smart enough to know you don't tell a girl she's one of the guys, even if that was how it felt.

But he had to say something, so he said, "The best part was when they broke in to steal the painting."

"Genius. Harpo turns on the flashlight to *look* for the flashlight? Pure comic genius."

"It was an ugly painting."

"Of course it was ugly, but that's irrelevant," she said, then dropping her voice an octave, wiggling an invisible cigar, she added, "And speaking of elephants, I once shot an elephant in my pajamas—"

"How he got in your pajamas you'll never know. I was sitting right here when he said it."

She paused, and he watched her watch the blank screen,

the look in her eyes changing. Then she said, "That's what we should do."

"Get in your pajamas?"

She pinched his arm.

"Okay, okay. Only kidding."

"Don't be like that."

"Fine."

"But we should do it."

Sawyer thought through the joke before he answered. "Shoot an elephant?"

"Steal a painting."

"Oh, yeah. That's a *brilliant* idea. Let's go."

"We could *so* do it."

"*Sure*. We'll just run over to the closest mansion, wait for them to throw a party for an African explorer, then grab the painting during the big dance number. I've got a flashlight in the trunk of my car."

She gave him a look that made him laugh, only she didn't laugh.

"Breaking into somebody's house is not all that hard and not all that cool."

"And breaking into a museum is . . . ?"

"Definitely hard and definitely cool."

"You've been watching too many movies."

"True," she said, climbing over the back of the couch. "But it's still a good idea."

She went to the kitchen and he heard the fridge open and shut, heard the ice dropping in the glass and the *fizz-click* of a diet cream soda can popping open. He waited till she came back, sitting cross-legged in the white leather chair, then he said, "Stealing a painting isn't going to make you famous."

"It might if I get caught. I'd get my picture in the paper. Probably front page. It'd be a mug shot, but that could still be cute. Ever see that one of Paris Hilton? Hot."

"I think there'd be more to it than that."

"Oh, for sure. The TV news would show me doing the perp walk, you know, when you go from the police van to the court house?"

"I take it you wouldn't cover your face."

"Are you kidding? I'd smile and say something clever every day. But nothing rude, you know what I mean? And I'd look good in an orange jumpsuit too, so there's that."

"I can't believe you're sitting here planning what you'd do if you got caught."

Grace laughed. "I wouldn't get caught."

"Because you wouldn't do something so stupid to begin with."

"No. Because getting away with it would be easy."

He nodded, playing along. She couldn't be serious. "Of course it is. I mean, stealing diamonds, *that's* hard. Paintings? Piece'a cake."

"A big diamond heist is next to impossible. What are you going to do, a smash-and-grab at a mall store? The big diamonds, the *really* big ones, they're all in the Smithsonian or some Saudi prince's dog's collar. You're not getting near those. And even if you do, you'll get caught for sure. Art theft is different. They don't get caught. What, you don't believe me? You're the one that wants to be an actuary. Look it up, Mr. I-Take-My-Share-of-Risks."

So he did. Googled it on his phone, thumbed through the suggested webpages, skimming enough to see that she was right. Sort of.

She watched him searching. "I'm betting they get away with it ninety-five percent of the time."

"Closer to eighty percent."

"Those are great odds."

"Not for everybody."

"Because not everybody knows what they're doing."

Done searching, he checked his phone for texts from

Zoë. There weren't any. "It isn't going to make you rich, either, you know. Even if you did get away with it, who you going to sell it to?"

"I wouldn't sell it."

"You couldn't hang it up in your room. Somebody sees it, you're busted. And you know your parents would start with the questions."

"There would be no questions. And I wouldn't hang it up."

"Don't tell me you'd burn it."

Her mouth dropped open. "Do I look crazy to you?"

He didn't answer.

"Burn it? You must think I'm insane to even *imagine* I'd do something evil like that. Is that what you think of me? That *I* would do something so—"

"You can't sell it and you can't hang it up," he said, cutting her off before she got too wound up. "What would you do with it?"

She smiled. "I'd return it."

"That makes no sense. Why steal it in the first place if you're gonna return it?"

She took a long, slow sip of her soda, then said, "Stealing a painting is cool. Returning it is even cooler."

"Okay, that's just stupid."

"You sneak back into the place you stole it from and put it right back where it was. That's amazingly cool."

"It's amazingly dumb."

"Then one day they come in, there it is, safe and sound. And with it, maybe on the wall or on a table, a calling card from the thief. 'Thanks for the loan— signed, The Mad Hatter.'"

"The Mad Hatter?"

"Just an example."

"Oh, good. I didn't want to think you'd do something crazy like use that name."

"You can't simply drop it off at the front desk."

"You could leave it someplace where the police would find it."

"What fun would *that* be?"

"Probably not as much fun as going to jail."

"I told you, I wouldn't get caught."

"What about fingerprints? DNA? They'd find you in a day, tops."

She laughed again. "And you think *I* watch too many movies? Say I was stupid enough to leave a fingerprint—what are they gonna match it to? My school

ID? And where they gonna get my DNA?"

"I don't know how they do it. Maybe they find a hair—"

"Great! Then all they have to do is test every dark-haired person in the state. Naturally, they'll start with me . . ."

"Fine. You get away with it—"

"Told you I would."

"—why would you bother to do it in the first place?"

She uncrossed her legs and leaned forward, her electric eyes looking right into his, saying each word slowly, clearly.

"Because it would be fun."

"Fun? You think breaking into a museum and stealing a painting, and then breaking back in to return it would be fun?"

"Yes. I do."

She wasn't kidding.

He didn't know how he knew, but he knew it.

She was serious.

Scary serious.

Actually do it serious.

Great.

"What are you doing for the next hour?" she said.

Leave right now. Stand up, walk out, get back home, don't even say good-bye. Get as far from Grace as possible.

That was one option.

"I need you to drive me somewhere."

That was another.

CHAPTER

13

SAWYER HAD NEVER been inside the William C. Wood Memorial Library before. It was a good forty minutes from his house—twenty-five from Grace's aunt's apartment—on the main street of a village, across the line where suburban became rural.

It was a big brick building, with white columns and white framed windows and a big wooden staircase right by the front door that creaked when you climbed the steps. It had once been the home of the Wood family when people lived in houses like that. Now it was a library, but it still had the rooms it had had when it was a house. The reference section was in the parlor, across the hall in the old dining room were history, science, and art. In the rear of the house, where the kitchen would have been if they had a kitchen in the house back then, were the computers and the copiers and the checkout desk. There were fluorescent lights hanging from the high ceilings and READ posters on the walls showing celebrities with books, a few framed pictures and WHERE TO FIND IT signs, just like any library, but with the fireplaces and the wallpaper it still felt like a house.

Grace had led the way, picking a small, round table, taking over half of it, piling it with books. He sat in the table's other chair and watched her work.

"Here's a really nice Cézanne," she said, tapping the full-color picture of a wobbly-looking barn next to a wobbly-looking mountain. "But it's at the Met in New York City."

"Figures. You find a painting you want to steal and it's in the wrong town."

"You're not being very supportive."

"I'm sorry," he said, checking his phone. Still no texts. That wasn't unusual, but if Zoë had texted he wanted to text back right away. Better that than dealing with all the questions later. Grace kept all the books on her side of the table, so he glanced around the room as they talked. "What kind of painting are you looking for?"

"Not sure yet. I like the Impressionists, but who doesn't, right?"

"Right . . ."

"I used to be big into Surrealism. Melting clocks, people with apples for heads. But it got kinda predictable—"

"Apples for heads. Definitely predictable."

"I *love* Duchamp, but I'm not going to steal a urinal."

"Okay, I have no idea what you're talking about."

"I guess what I'm looking for is a painting with lots of color, not realistic but nothing too out there—"

Sawyer scanned the walls. "Uh-huh."

"Not a still life. No bowls of fruit."

"Of course not."

"And something *different*, you know? Exotic."

"Exotic. Sure." The small one by the fire alarm.

"Like a tropical island or a Chinese temple or a bullfight—"

"How do you feel about camels?"

"Cute animal, awful cigarette."

"How about paintings with camels? Say, camels in an oasis with Arabs and a tent and a couple dogs."

She looked up from the book. "Where's it at? The Louvre?"

He pointed with his chin. "The wall."

She spun around in her chair and as soon as she saw the painting she gave a little gasp.

"It's no Cézanne, but it's not Surrealist, either," he said, wondering if he was close to being right.

"Oh, it's *beautiful*," she said, and there was something soft in her voice he hadn't heard before. Eyes locked on the painting, she crossed the small room, head tilted back so she could see it. She stood there for a minute, mouth open, not saying anything, then, almost too quiet to hear, she said, "See if the coast is clear."

"Whoa, you're not going to—"

"*Shhhhh*. I just wanna check something. You see anybody?"

He slid his chair back and stood, careful not to make a sound, then leaned out into the hall. An old librarian was showing an even older man how to create an online account.

"Go ahead. You've got time."

Using the tips of her pinkie fingers, Grace angled the bottom of the painting away from the wall and waited. "No alarms yet, that's good." On her toes, she looked underneath. "No wires, no contacts. Geez, it's not even bolted down." As she lifted the painting off the hook, Sawyer felt a cold, electric tingle roll from his stomach to his crotch, and as she walked toward him with the painting, he felt his knees give a bit.

"Check it out," she said, holding it up for him to see.

It was about the size of his laptop, with a dusty wooden frame and a tarnished brass nameplate that said G. RAVLIN—MOROCCAN MARKET. It looked out of focus, the paint brushed on thick, the details all blurred over. Were they men or women? Or both? Was that a rifle or a stick? There were camels, either three with five legs or five with three. The colors were way off—the sand was mustard yellow and white, the animals looked more red than brown, and the shadows were blue and pink. The whole thing seemed sloppy and rushed and he didn't like it, but the way Grace was oohing and aahing, he figured it was best not to say anything.

"It's perfect," she said. "Impressionist, early nineteen hundreds, maybe even the late eighteen hundreds."

"And you know this how?"

"Art history class. Or don't you have that over at ritzy East High?"

They might, he didn't know. Besides, it sounded like a fluff course and you shouldn't have courses like that on your transcripts. At least that's what his parents said.

"What do you think, ten pounds?" She handed it to him, and he felt that tingle amp up.

"Lighter. Five, tops. The frame's made out of pine. It only looks heavy."

"Pine? How can you tell?"

"You're not the only one who knows things."

"So tell me, Woody, how hard would it be to take the frame off?"

He turned it upside down and checked the corners. "This thing's on good. You'd need a bunch of tools and you'd probably bust the frame. Or poke a hole in the painting. I'd say leave it on."

"Fine, we'll leave it on."

It took a second, but it sunk in.

"We?"

"Whatever. Okay, here's what you do—"

"You're taking it *now*?"

"Of course not. Too easy."

"Easy? Let me guess. We need a plan."

She smiled up at him. "You're catching on. First I have to check something. How we doing?"

Holding the painting to the side, Sawyer leaned into the hall. He could hear the librarian explaining the difference between user names and passwords and the way she was saying it, he could tell she wasn't getting through. "We're still good," he said, and looked over to the table where Grace was emptying out his backpack.

"What are you doing?" He wanted to yell but somehow kept it to a clenched-jaw whisper. "I'm not stealing that painting."

"Relax, I'm just checking for size. I don't want to be here at three in the morning and find out I brought the wrong bag." She stacked up his textbooks and binders and his laptop on the table, then held open the backpack.

"No, wait," he said. "You've gotta unzip it more."

"I can't. It's stuck on some of the trim."

Sawyer handed Grace the painting, then turned the empty bag sideways and was feeling for the zipper tab when the librarian said, "Can I help you with that?"

She was standing in the doorway, younger than Sawyer had assumed, and a hell of a lot quieter. Sawyer felt his hands start to shake and his throat tighten, and he felt the frame of the painting brush against his leg as Grace slid it in next to the chair.

"Those can be trouble if they jam," the librarian said, stepping toward the table.

"I think I got it," Sawyer said, yanking the zipper all

the way up, forever wedging the fabric into the plastic teeth. "Perfect."

The librarian kept coming.

"Looks like you two are stealing a painting."

What the librarian really said was "working on an art project," but with the roar in his ears, it didn't sound that way to Sawyer. Grace, all casual, said no, it was for a history class, as he stood there, hands still on the damn backpack, his knee knocking against the pine frame, the pine frame knocking against the oak leg of the table, a telltale *tap, tap, tap* the librarian *had* to hear. Then Grace was saying something about Renaissance portraits, spinning one of the books around to show the librarian what she meant, the librarian bending over the table, looking, saying yes, of course, but there are better books on the subject, then the librarian and Grace walking over to one of the tall shelves, their backs to Sawyer, who wanted to run, who was ready to run, but who for some uncontrollable reason did the opposite, sliding the chair away from the table and sitting down, hopping the chair forward until his rumbling stomach was touching, and, without looking, swinging the now massive, impossibly huge painting up onto his lap, balancing it on his knees, then popping up on his toes till the frame whapped up flat against the underside of the table just as the librarian and Grace turned around, Grace asking the librarian if she *wanted to sit down* and help pick out a painting that's a good example of whatever story she'd been selling, the librarian saying she'd love to, but that she'd better see how Mr. Stewart is doing with the computer, and then she was gone and Sawyer's heart started to beat again.

"Very impressive, Mr. Bond," Grace said, taking the painting off his lap. She gave a glance at the doorway, then walked over and hung the painting on the hook, stepping back to see if it was straight.

Sawyer sat at the table, massaging the cramps out of his calves. "That was close."

"That was better than close," Grace said, trying to force his textbooks through the tiny opening in his ruined backpack. "That was fun."

Hours later—after dropping Grace off at her aunt's apartment, eating dinner, doing his homework, and talking to Zoë—Sawyer thought of something that scared the hell out of him.

It *was* fun.

CHAPTER 14

"KNOCK, KNOCK," SAWYER'S father said, rapping a knuckle on the door as he pushed it open. If it had been closed all the way his father would've waited until Sawyer said come in. He'd been a teenager once so he knew better. But the rule was if the door was open a crack, it might as well have been open all the way, so knocking and coming in at the same time was cool.

Sawyer was at his desk, computer screen dark, phone off, textbook open, calculator fired up, and eyes glazed over. It wasn't sticking, but not from a lack of effort. He looked up from his all-wrong equations.

"Don't forget, set your alarm early. St. Mary's starts serving at five."

Sawyer slumped down against the back of the chair,

turned his head up to the ceiling and closed his eyes. He *had* forgotten. He sighed and mumbled something that he didn't want to say out loud.

"You made a commitment, Sawyer. You know how I feel about that."

No, he didn't. When it came to commitments, his father was all over the place, honoring some—like the one to his golf league—as if his life depended on it, ignoring others—like his promise to help with the landscaping at the church—as if someone else had said it. But when it came to commitments his father made for him—like working the soup kitchen at St. Mary's two days a week and every holiday—Sawyer knew exactly how his father felt. And Sawyer knew what he wanted to say about that commitment and the coming four twenty wake-up. Instead he said, "Who would want soup at five in the morning?"

"Very funny. You know it's not soup. But even if it was, these people don't have jobs, some don't have *anything*. Don't they at least deserve a good, hot breakfast?"

Yeah, of course they did. Stupid question. But if they didn't have jobs, couldn't they eat a little later? It wasn't like they were going to be late for work. Sawyer went over to his bed, resetting the alarm since he knew his father would stand there till he did.

"You're not working on precalculus, are you?"

"There's a big test Thursday." He double-checked the alarm. Four-frickin'-twenty a.m. Damn.

His father gave a you-don't-get-it headshake combined with a what-am-I-going-to-do-with-this-kid eye roll. "You're already accepted. You don't have to worry about this class."

"I know, it's just that some of the other schools I'm looking at require an extra year of math and—"

"Sawyer, why are you wasting your time looking at other schools? You're in at Wembly, I told you that."

"They were on my list and I wanted to see if I could get accepted. Some of them offer decent scholarships."

The long sigh. "I'm sure you'd get in, son. You're a bright guy and you've got a lot on your transcript. But there's no sense spending time filling out applications for schools you're not going to go to even if they *do* accept you. And what are you going to get for a scholarship? Two grand a year? That won't cover anything. And there's application fees, too. What, like, fifty bucks a pop?"

"Something like that."

"That's a lot of money to be expecting us to pay just so you can see if you would have made it in."

"I was going to pay for them myself," Sawyer said, though he had expected his parents to pay.

"At minimum wage? You'd use your whole paycheck applying to two schools."

His father was wrong. He didn't make that much, not this time of the year, anyway.

"You've already been accepted to Wembly. Focus on your other classes, finish strong there. And talk to your counselors about dropping precalc. If they give you any grief let me know. One call and I'll get it taken care of."

Sawyer sat back down at his desk. The papers in front of him were covered with numbers and symbols and equations he only half understood, the answers on his homework assignment guesses at best. His schedule would be easy without it, and he wouldn't have that daily headache that came every time Mr. Young started talking.

If he went to Wembly, he wouldn't have to worry about precalc.

And since he'd be staying here in town, he could keep his job at Mike's Ice Cream.

And since he'd be living at home, in the same room

he'd been in since he was five, he wouldn't have to deal with wild all-night dorm parties he'd heard so much about.

And since Zoë was going to Wembly too, they wouldn't have to break up, he wouldn't have to deal with that whole dating hassle or worry about meeting girls or finding a new girlfriend or several girlfriends, girls from other towns, other states, maybe even other countries, girls to hang out with, watch movies with, fool around and stuff with. Yes sir, with Zoë right there with him— reminding him what to do and what not to do, keeping an eye on him all the time, letting everybody know that they were dating, *dating since tenth grade*—he wouldn't have to worry about any of that. He wouldn't have—

"Earth to Sawyer," his father said, laughing as he said it. "I sure hope you don't space out like that when you're driving."

"Oh, sorry. I was just thinking about what you said."

"Nothing to think about. Just let me know if you need me to call. Now get some sleep. Five o'clock comes early, and you gave your word."

15

GOD, HE HATED these stupid quizzes.

The questions were ridiculous, the answers made no sense, and you couldn't fail if you wanted to. Yet somehow he kept picking the wrong answer.

"Question six. Which best describes your relationship: (a) a glass of water, (b) a book, (c) an umbrella, or (d) ice cream?"

See?

"Do I get a hint?"

Zoë thought it over as she flipped to the back of the *Cosmo* to peek at the answers. "Okay. What do you think of when you think of water?"

"Wet?"

"No. What color is it?"

"There is no color."

"So what color is that?"

"I don't know what—"

"'Choosing water means that you value the *transparency* of your relationship,'" she read. "'You and your lover hide nothing from each other and, like the elemental simplicity of water, you need add nothing to it to make it complete. It is pure and timeless in nature and like the natural world it requires' blah, blah, blah . . . anyway, it goes on like that. Too Mother Earthy for me. You didn't pick that one, did you?"

He said no, of course not, wondering if it was accurate to call them lovers.

"Now the next one, a book, that's easy." She flicked her wrist and the magazine flipped back to where her thumb marked the answers. "Yeah, like I figured. 'As the pages tell the story, so do your actions move the plot of your relationship along . . .' They use that answer in every quiz. Which one do you think we're like?"

He considered the remaining choices. "An umbrella?"

"An umbrella? *Seriously,* Sawyer? An *umbrella*?"

It was wrong—obviously—but he felt he had to defend his choice. "It keeps you protected when things are bad . . ."

Zoë shook her head, amazed at his ignorance. "'An

umbrella relationship is disposable and one-sided, based on fulfilling short-term, self-centered needs.'" She looked over at him, her eyes narrowing. "You don't think I'm self-centered, do you?"

"Yeah, right," he said, playing it off the way he always played it off whenever she said stuff like that. You don't go out with somebody for two years without learning a few things. "That's why I was going to say that we're like ice cream."

"I *knew* you'd say that," she said, giddy-happy, snuggling in closer, as close as she would on the couch with her parents ten quick steps away. "That's what *I* picked too." She flipped and read. "'Ice-cream couples are wild and spontaneous, dishing out the fun when they are with friends but happiest when they get to melt alone together.' Aww. That's *so* us."

That wasn't what Sawyer thought. What came to him were words like *cold* and *headaches* and *sticky*, and how ice cream made him think of work, of the boring hours that dragged by and how sometimes he thought he'd be stuck behind that counter for the rest of his life and how that made him want to quit right there but knew he couldn't because that would disappoint his parents.

That's what he thought of when he thought of ice cream.

What he said was, "Yeah, it *is* us."

Then Zoë said how she didn't want ice cream but could really go for a Popsicle now, and for a second Sawyer thought she was hinting at something else he had seen in the magazine, something really wild, but no, she wanted a Popsicle, so the ice-cream couple headed upstairs to the fridge and spent a spontaneous dinner hour watching TV with her parents.

CHAPTER
16

IT WAS THE Xbox that got him thinking.

Everything was going like it always went—jumping in on a mission, moving through the warehouse or the factory or the palace, popping the enemy, supporting his teammates, getting killed, reviving, pushing on to the next level. Then there it was, this tiny speck of an idea, a ridiculous, sleep-deprived half thought that should have faded to nothing, that wouldn't stop growing, that wouldn't be ignored, and the more he tried to ignore it the more it pushed its way in, taking over, until it was all he could think about.

Life was a game.

He was Player One.

But someone else was working the controls.

Of course it was stupid. It was the kind of idea that made perfect sense when you were stoned or that came to you in the dark at three in the morning, like atoms being planets or Nostradamus being God, the kind of idea that evaporated in sunlight, that you wouldn't admit you had, not even to yourself. But when he was killed for the fifth time and finally logged out, there it was, stuck in the back of his mind, somewhere between precalc and college.

Sawyer didn't see her when he pulled into the parking lot of the 7-Eleven.

She said she'd be waiting out front, but it was a cold and dark mid-November night, and he knew she wouldn't be standing around outside. He was about to turn off his car when he spotted her coming out carrying two large Slurpees. He leaned over and unlocked the door, and she slid in, handing him one of the massive cups.

"Hope you like purple," Grace said, and balanced the second cup between her knees as she buckled her seatbelt.

"After green, blue, brown, and red it's my favorite."

"Thought so," she said, then looked over at him with an embarrassed smile. "Thanks for this."

"No problem," he said. "I was doing nothing anyway."

It was almost true. He had been working on pre-calculus—*again*—when she called, so it was like doing nothing since that's about what he got out of it. He didn't recognize the phone number and was going to ignore it, but on the sixth ring something clicked and he remembered.

She said hello, was he busy, could he do her a favor, could he give her a lift home, was he sure it wasn't too late.

It was ten forty on a school night and that meant he'd have to make up a decent story—*That new guy from school, the one with the neck brace? He got a flat in his church parking lot and he asked if I could help him out*—but he'd be there.

"I suppose you're wondering what a nice girl like me is doing in a parking lot in this part of town."

"Didn't cross my mind," he said, wondering what she was doing in a parking lot in this part of town. "Where to?"

"My house. You know the west side, where the Kmart is? Head that way." She took a long, brain-freezing sip of her drink, then said, "This is why I hate going out."

"Going out where?"

"It's not the where that's the problem. It's the who."

"You were on a *date*?"

"Try not to sound so surprised. Yes, I was on a *date*, as you call it. Probably the last one ever."

"For you or him?"

"Me, naturally. He'll get plenty. Until he starts getting all grabby. But then most girls probably like that stuff so, yeah, he'll still get plenty of dates."

Sawyer glanced over. "He didn't try anything, to like, you know—"

"Of course he did, Sherlock, but his mom taught him that no means no so he stopped. Too bad she didn't teach him that no also means drive the girl home."

Sawyer nodded. Guys like that gave every guy a bad name. But he *did* stop so maybe he wasn't a total jerk. "First time you went out with him?"

She laughed, and just like that, the tension in the air was broken, gone. "I don't get a lot of second dates. I *want* them, but I don't get them. It seems I'm *difficult* to get along with."

"Because you won't . . ." He let it trail off, not sure what it was she wouldn't do.

"That's part of it, yeah. But mostly guys say that I'm

hard to talk to. Go left here, it's quicker," she said, pointing.

Sawyer flicked on his directional.

Hard to talk to?

She had to be kidding.

She was the *easiest* person to talk to.

Sawyer turned left. He knew the main roads on the west side but that was it. He assumed she knew where she was taking him. They drove a mile in silence, then Sawyer said, "When I was in middle school, I couldn't talk to girls. I mean, yeah, I could *talk*, but I couldn't sit there and have a conversation, you know what I mean? I wouldn't know what to say, I'd mumble something, then I'd start to sweat—it really sucked."

Where in the hell did that come from? he thought.

"That's every guy in middle school," she said. "If they say it wasn't them, they're liars. But then most guys are liars, so there you go."

"Nice. I give you a ride and you call me a liar."

"*Most* guys, Sherlock, *most* guys. You're not most guys. If you were, I wouldn't have called you."

"You could have called one of your friends."

"I thought I did."

"You know what I mean. A girl friend."

"Like my BFF or something? Yeah, don't have many of those, either."

"Oh. Sorry."

"I'm not. They'd only want something from me when I'm famous."

"Or rich."

"Right. Rich and famous. You wait, then they'll be sorry."

What was it that Sandra's friend at West said about Grace? That she was a loser with no friends? Somebody even the geeks ignored? That was one way of looking at it.

"So, what were you doing when I called? You weren't with your girlfriend, were you? Hate to mess that up."

"No, I was studying for a test. Precalc." He shook his head. "I don't know why I bother."

"Yes, you do. You need it to get into college. Oh, don't look surprised, it's obvious. Why *else* would anybody take it? It's part of a big government plan to keep math teachers employed. You don't want them rioting in the streets, do you?"

"Maybe. Will the police need to use clubs and tear gas on them?"

"Ooh, I like the way you think. Veer to the right at

the light," she said, motioning with her straw. "I thought it was all decided that you were going to Wembly?"

"That's the plan for now."

"Sounds like you have other ideas."

Sawyer sipped his drink. "I *had* other ideas, but they all involved me passing precalc, and that means passing the test, and that ain't happening, so . . ."

"Turn right at the stop sign. When's the test?"

"Thursday."

"I'm down with all things calculi. Come over to my aunt's place tomorrow around three. I'll have you ready in an hour."

He laughed. "An hour? What good is that?"

"Trust me. Besides, I owe you for the ride."

"You don't owe me anything."

"I know, but it's the kind of thing you're supposed to say. This is the street."

He'd never been in this neighborhood before, but it was what everybody thought of when they said "west side." Tiny dirt lawns with tiny dirty houses, boxes with two windows to a side and door in the front. Baby-Boomer tracks—that's what his history teacher had called them—built after World War II or Vietnam or some other war for all the veterans coming home, eager to get married and start pumping out kids. It would have been crowded with two people, yet every house seemed to have four cars in a driveway meant for one.

He wanted to ask, but then he didn't want to know.

"Pull up anywhere."

"Which one's your house?"

"None of these. I'll cut through a few yards and go in through the back porch."

"You sure? I don't mind—"

"I start coming in the front door after all these years, it'll just feel strange."

Sawyer eased over to the curb and put the car in park.

"Sorry your date turned out so shitty."

"Eh. No big deal. Besides, it ended up okay."

Great. *Now* what? He didn't want to kiss her and he knew she didn't want to be kissed. It wasn't like that. It *should've* been, she was cute and he was a guy and they were alone in a dark car in a dark neighborhood, but it wasn't like that. He was glad it was that way, but he wasn't in a rush to see her go.

"Later." She unbuckled her seatbelt and turned to open the door.

"Wait a second. Can I ask you a question?"

"This isn't going to get weird, is it? Because I already had enough weird for one night."

"Say you were dating somebody—"

"It's a stretch, but go on."

"Would you want your relationship to be—"

"Now it's a *relationship*? Boy, that moved along fast."

He sighed a fake sigh. "Can I just ask the damn question?"

"Sorry. Go on. Would I want my relationship to be . . . ?"

"To be more like an umbrella or more like ice cream?"

She blinked. *"What?"*

"More like an umbrella or more like ice cream. Which one?"

"Is this one of those bad SAT questions?"

"It's from some magazine. *Cosmopolitan.*"

"Cosmo, huh?"

"It's Zoë's. She likes to—"

"Spare me the details. What are my choices again?"

"An umbrella or ice cream."

"That's easy. An umbrella. Can I go now?" She opened the door and the light went on.

"Hold on. Why an umbrella?"

She got out and held the door open, leaning into the light.

"If you've got two people and one umbrella, you have to stick close together if you want it to work."

The door swung closed, the light went out, and before his eyes adjusted, she was gone.

CHAPTER

17

ZOË SLAMMED HER locker shut.

"What do you mean you can't drive me home?"

He knew this question was coming. Knew it the moment Grace said she could help him pass his precalculus exam. He had all night and most of the day to be ready with an answer, but when it finally came, five minutes after the last bell, he was still unprepared.

She knew his work schedule, so that was out, and the soup kitchen was only open at ungodly hours around dawn. If he said he was staying after school for something, she'd say she'd hang out there, and if he said he had to go somewhere—the mall to pick up whatever—she'd want to go. He was this close to saying *Oh wait, I can drive you home after all*, when he said, "You know the old guy I work with at Mike's? Francis McGillicutty? Yeah, well he used to be a math professor. He's going to help me with precalc."

She wasn't buying it.

"What does he know? He can't make change for a twenty without a calculator."

"He's cautious, that's all."

"Where'd he teach?"

"Notre Dame." *Notre Dame?*

"And now he scoops ice cream for a living?"

"He's retired. It gives him something to do."

"Why don't you just ask Mr. Young? He's your teacher, that's his job."

"I'm not getting it with him."

"Oh, so you're going to get it with an old guy. That sounds sick."

He rubbed the back of his neck where the headache was starting. "You want me to fail?"

"You might as well. You're already accepted at Wembly. It's not like they're going to change their minds."

"I'm not going to risk it," he said, and then he knew what to say. "That's where you're going to be, and I have to make sure I'm there too. And that means passing this stupid test and *that* means spending a few hours at an old guy's house on the west side."

Perfect.

She made a face, softened it, then made another. "Fine. But how am I supposed to get home?"

"Come with me. I'm sure he won't mind if you wait. You can talk to his wife. I'll drive you home after. Shouldn't be more than two or three hours."

"Yeah, right." She had her phone out, her thumb a blur on the keypad. "I'll catch a ride with Renée." She gave him a lightning-quick kiss—her standard public display of affection—said "Love ya," turned around, and headed to the parking lot.

Sawyer watched her go, enjoying the view.

"I brought my textbook, some notes, this review guide—never opened—calculator, the last quiz we took. Fifty-two percent, thank you. A Mountain Dew for me and a diet cream soda for you."

Sawyer unloaded his backpack—a new one with zippers that worked—on the kitchenette table, careful not to drop anything on Grace's laptop. She ignored all but the soda, popped open the can, and said, "How good's your hearing?"

"My *hearing*?"

"Don't tell me you didn't hear that, or we're in trouble."

"I heard you. But what does that have to do with anything?"

"That's how you're going to pass this test." She took a sip of her diet cream soda—*who drinks that crap?*—leaning against the fridge as he sat down. "Do you wear glasses?"

"Have you ever seen me with glasses?"

She shrugged. "I don't know, you could have contacts."

"No. No glasses, no contacts."

"Good. It's time you start. Put that stuff away," she said, waving a hand over the notebooks and papers.

"Aren't we going to need them?"

"I don't see why."

"You said you'd help me pass the test."

"I know what I said." She picked up a shoebox off the counter and brought it to the table, sitting in the only other chair.

"You were going to teach me calculus."

"Silly rabbit. I can't teach you that."

"I thought you were good at it."

"I'm *great* at it. I just can't teach it. Not in one day, anyway."

Sawyer thought of Zoë, stuck riding home with Renée and how—*somehow*—she'd hold it against him later. Not good. "Then why'd you have me come over? To watch another stupid movie?"

"I'd be careful what I say if I were you. You need me to pass that test."

"You just said you can't teach me calculus."

"Passing the test has nothing to do with you learning precalc." She took the lid off the shoebox, shuffled some things around he couldn't see, and pulled out a pair of old-man glasses. Thick black frames and a fat wad of black duct tape wrapped around the bridge, another wad holding one of the arms on the frame. "Here. Put these on."

He laughed as she handed them to him. "Ooooh. Are they *magic* glasses?"

"Yeah, smartass, they are."

He went to put them on and stopped. "There's a wire or something sticking out of the frame. Here, by the ear part."

"Don't pull on it. Geez. It took me forever to get that

taped down. And it's not a wire, it's a tube."

Sawyer held the glasses up to the light. A thin strip of black electrical tape ran along the inside of the frame from the wad on the hinge to the tip. The clear plastic tube was under the tape, except for the end that dangled down an extra inch.

"Check out the front. That's the best part."

"The tape job?"

"Look closer."

He did, and he wouldn't have seen it if he hadn't. A round, flat piece of glass, smaller than a match head and as black as the frame. "Is this a lens?"

"It's a five-point-eight gigahertz pinhole webcam."

Compact and smooth, it looked expensive. "Where'd you get it?"

"Do you *really* want to know?"

"I guess not."

"You guessed right. And see this part here? It's a sound tube from a hearing aid. On a full charge it'll last four hours. It's supposed to be good for up to five hundred feet, more than that if you're outside. That ought to be plenty."

She didn't have to tell him the rest.

"No way." He set the glasses on the table.

"What do you mean?"

"I'm not wearing them to school."

"Why not? They're brilliant. Okay, maybe a bit nerdy, but that's sorta in now. And you don't have to wear them all day, just for the test."

"There's no way I'm going to wear these."

"You're not going to get caught. No one would ever suspect it. That's why it's brilliant."

"It's cheating."

"Oh, please."

"I mean it. It's cheating."

"Who cares?"

"I do. It's wrong."

"Wrong is clubbing baby seals. This?" She slapped the side of his textbook. "This is a game. A hoop you've gotta jump through."

"And so the glasses are what, Air Jordans?"

"Yeah, sure. You need an edge to win this game."

"It's not a game."

"At least try them on."

"No. I'm not going to wear them."

"I worked all night on those," she said, and for the first time since he knew her, she looked sad. He should've put them on, let her show off, let her explain how she figured it all out and where she got the parts, but he knew he couldn't. Because if he did—if he tried them on and they really did work, if they really were brilliant—he knew he'd be wearing them when he took the test.

"I gotta go," he said, standing up, loading his backpack.

"Hold on a second. Look, okay, maybe I was pushing a little hard, but I know how much you want to pass and I figured I could help and it would be fun—"

"Right, fun. That's what it's all about."

She looked at him and smiled, sort of. "Part of it."

"Sometimes you have to do things that aren't fun at all, and taking this test is one of them."

"Now you sound like your parents."

"You've never met them."

"Tell me I'm wrong. Tell me that's not them talking."

He slung his backpack over his shoulder. "I gotta go."

"If you change your mind . . ."

"I'm not going to."

She walked him through the apartment, then stood on the landing as he went down the stairs and out the front entrance. He heard her shout "Good luck."

CHAPTER
18

THE DOOR WAS shut, so when his father knocked, Sawyer leaned over from his desk and let him in.

"Saw the light under the door. It's after midnight, you know."

"Yeah, I know," Sawyer said. "I'm almost finished."

"A little late for homework, isn't it? You're supposed to get this done right after school."

"It's not homework. I've got a test tomorrow," he said, and then without thinking he added, "precalc."

The dramatic sigh, the disgusted head shake.

"Didn't I tell you to drop that class?"

"You said something about it, yeah."

"Are they giving you grief in the guidance office? I'll

call them tomorrow morning, get it taken care of, get you out of it. They can't—"

"I haven't gone there yet."

A surprised pause.

"Haven't gone where?"

"The guidance office."

A longer pause.

"Okay. Why not?"

Sawyer tossed his pencil on the desk. "I think I can pass the class."

His father shifted his weight, a shoulder against the doorframe, his hand still on the knob, his thumb tapping out a steady, calming beat. "I thought we made it clear why you should drop it."

"Well, I thought it was better if I stayed," Sawyer said, then surprised himself by looking up at his father, meeting his stare.

A tense silence, not long but deep.

"I suppose you think you have a good reason."

"Yeah," he said. "I can pass."

His father nodded, but Sawyer knew he didn't agree. Then his father said, "It's not worth busting your ass over."

"I don't mind the work."

"It's not that. Look at yourself. You're staying up late to cram for a test you don't have to take. You *do* understand that, don't you?"

"Yeah, I get it."

"All that effort you're putting into one class. Put that to work in your other classes and you can raise those grades up, improve your GPA."

"What difference does it make? I'm already accepted."

"It's not about the grades, son, it's about effort. You should always give it your best."

Sawyer held up the evidence, a paper covered with numbers and half-finished equations.

"This is different and you know it," his father said, that parental tone creeping into his voice.

For a second Sawyer thought about arguing the point, telling him why it *wasn't* different, why it was the kind of thing they'd always said he *should* do, quoting a few of his father's favorite lines about commitment and hard work. But that wasn't the fight to take on at midnight, ten hours before the test. So instead he said, "I'm gonna pass."

His father didn't laugh, but he came close.

"Seriously. I feel really, I don't know, confident."

Sawyer *did* feel something, and maybe it was confidence. But he doubted it.

"That's nice, son. But do you really think squeaking by on one test is going to make a difference?"

"I was planning to do better than squeaking by."

"What, a C? That's not going to change your overall grade enough to matter."

"No, better than a C."

"So a C-plus? B-minus, maybe? That's still not enough."

His father was right and Sawyer knew it. The extra points would barely budge his average. As for getting a B-minus, he'd be lucky to get a D.

Sawyer knew all this, and he still said, "I'm gonna ace the test."

His father took in a slow, deep breath. "Look, son, the best grade you got so far this year was a C, and the rest of the time you've been bouncing around, what, a fifty-percent average? It's not that I don't want you to do well, you know that. I just don't want to see you spending time in your senior year worrying about a class you don't need to take. Now, do I want to see you get an A? Yes. I'd love it. But is it realistic? You might do okay, but come on, we both know you're not going to get an A on that test."

Sawyer smiled. Go big or go home. "Wanna bet?"

"Geez, son, I *just* got finished explaining—"

"If I get an A on the test, you leave me alone about the class for the rest of the year," Sawyer said, his voice different now too, relaxed and confident.

"Now you're being childish."

"If I don't get an A, I'll drop the class."

His father smiled at that. "Is that it? Is that the bet?"

"Yeah," Sawyer said. "And just so you know, if I ace the test, I'm going to apply to other schools."

"What's wrong with Wembly?"

"Nothing's wrong with it. I want to try other schools, that's all. See what happens."

"You're setting yourself up to be embarrassed, you realize that, right?"

"Maybe."

"Okay," his father said, chuckling as he said it. "If that's the way you want to play it. I'll take your bet. Just so we're clear, anything less than an A, and we're done discussing precalculus. And if, by chance, you get an A, I'll support your decision to at least *apply* to other schools."

"What about the application fees?"

"Fine, fine," his father said, and now he was laughing. "Fees, too. But I don't want to hear any whining about it later if things don't go your way."

"No. It's cool."

"All right, then." His father reached out his hand and Sawyer shook it, firm but not too strong, the way his father had taught him to shake, a sucker bet still a bet.

"Enough cramming for one night. If you don't know it by now, you'll never get it." His father left, pulling the door shut behind him.

Ten minutes later, as he lay in bed, Sawyer sent a text message.

CHAPTER

19

"OKAY, YOU KNOW the drill. Everything off your desks but your calculator and your pens. And no pencils this time, right, Alicia? Very funny. Just don't use it on the test."

Mr. Young was making his way down the aisle, handing out the packets. Four pages of questions, double-sided, stapled at the top left corner, five pages of official blank paper to SHOW ALL WORK clipped to each test.

"Remember, it's a B day. You'll have the full ninety minutes, so pace yourselves. There's plenty of time. And do I have to say anything about keeping your eyes on your own papers?"

Sawyer took the glasses out of his shirt pocket. They were as big and ugly as they were the day before, maybe bigger and uglier. He flicked out the tape-covered arms and took a deep breath.

Less than a minute after he had hit Send last night, he'd gotten a reply.

NP meet u at Starbucks by your school 7AM

And she was there when he pulled up, a table by the window, laptop open, checking a celebrity gossip page. He walked over to her and she smiled. She didn't give him any grief, didn't go off on an I-told-you-so rant, didn't get all smartass on him, just gave him the glasses.

Where's the power switch?

They're on already.

What about the volume?

Isn't any. Cup your hand over your ear like this or you won't be able to hear me.

How good will you be able to see?

Good enough. So watch where you're looking.

Anything else?

Yeah. Trust me.

"If you finish early that's a good sign you made a *lot* of mistakes. Go back, double-check your work. Wrong answers can still earn you partial credit but I have to be able to read it, so write legibly."

Sawyer looked at the glasses, at the lumps of black tape, at the clear plastic tube that stuck out so damn obvious now, the whole thing an impossible joke.

He could put them on, find out they didn't even work, all that sweating for nothing.

Or they could work and everything could be going fine. Until Mr. Young figured it out and he got busted.

Or they could work and Mr. Young wouldn't notice, and he could learn that Grace was no better at precalc than he was.

Or he could put them back in his pocket, do the test on his own. And fail.

Or it would work and—

"Cheaters," Mr. Young said, standing next to Sawyer's desk, looking right at him as he said it.

Sawyer didn't move.

"Cheaters," he said again, nodding at the glasses in Sawyer's hands.

"I, uh, I can—"

"That's what they used to call reading glasses. Cheaters. Not prescription but still a help."

Sawyer forced a smile and put the glasses on. Fast. "I never heard that before."

Mr. Young dropped a pile of papers on the desk, blank-side up. "That pair's seen better days."

"Yeah. Kinda rough. They were uh, my, uh grandpa's. My mom's dad. Before he died."

"Well, I hope they bring you luck."

"Me too," Sawyer said, thinking about his grandpa and how he'd never wear such ugly glasses. And how surprised Grandpa would be to hear that he was dead.

So that was it, he was wearing them now.

He glanced up when Mr. Young asked the class if they had any last questions, but everything was fuzzy so he looked back down and focused on the magnified paperclip.

"Okay, your time starts . . . now. Good luck."

Sawyer turned the papers over and wrote his name on the line in the upper left-hand corner. Then he skimmed the first ten questions, looking for an easy one to start with.

He didn't see any.

He folded back the page and ran his eyes down the next set.

Even worse.

He was flipping the packet over and was halfway down when he heard a mosquito by his left ear. He went to flick it away when he remembered. He cupped his hand over his ear and leaned to the side, all casual.

Nothing.

He adjusted his hand, feeling for the plastic tube with his thumb, maneuvering it into his ear.

Nothing.

He pushed his hand tight against the side of his head and could hear the wet *swish-thump, swish-thump* of his pulse in the roaring silence.

He tilted his head—a little, not enough to make it noticeable—toward the windows one row away, toward the faculty parking lot and the narrow grassy area that nobody used, toward the chain-link fence and the Starbucks that Grace had assumed was less than five hundred feet away but that was probably more like ten or twelve miles, too far for her puny laptop and the lousy shared Wi-Fi—

"Are you going to start this test or what?"

He snapped his head up.

Mr. Young was at his desk, reading his iPad.

"Whoa, not so fast. Makes me dizzy."

It was faint, but clear, and he pressed his hand tighter, holding her voice in.

"You seemed surprised to hear from me. I can go if you'd rather be alone. No? Okay, then back to page one.

We'll start with the simple ones."

He looked at the test paper and froze, afraid to lose the connection.

"Is that how you normally sit in class, all stiff like that? Relax, Max, you've got to act natural. Just do what you'd normally do when you take a test."

He wrote "I PANIC" in half-inch caps on the scrap paper.

"Cute. But don't do that. Don't write me notes. Well, don't panic, either, but definitely don't write notes."

He drew a question mark.

"Because you have to turn in the scrap paper and if it's covered with notes, you'll have some explaining to do. Keep your head steady. That's good. Chin down just a bit. Too much. Perfect. All right, page one, please."

Sawyer flipped back and stared at the first question.

"'Factor this expression: X to the fourth plus eight X to the second plus twelve.' Could he start us off any easier? We simplify this . . . X squared . . . write that down . . . then X to the fourth . . . multiples of twelve that add up to eight—duh, six and two. I hope he doesn't expect you to show how you got *that*. And your answer is X squared plus six times X squared plus two. No, get rid of that multiplication sign. Yeah, that one. Put them in parentheses. You *do* know parentheses, right? Just wondering. Okay, done. Now, question two . . ."

It felt familiar, some of it, anyway, and there were a couple times when he knew what she was going to say before she said it. But there were more times when what he would have written was nothing at all like what she told him to put down.

"'Question ten. X to the fourth plus sixty-four equals . . .' Oh, this is interesting. . . ."

His hand was sweating against his ear. He left it there, afraid that if he moved it the faint buzzing whisper would somehow echo across the room or disappear into cyberia. He looked up to check the clock between answers since that's the kind of thing he'd do during a test, and every time he did, she would make some comment about roller coasters or drunken dancing.

They were halfway through page two when Grace said, "Hi, can I get a caramel macchiato and one of these yummy brownies?" and for five minutes he listened to the gurgling hiss of the espresso machine and to Grace as she hummed along to a Skye Sweetnam song that played in the background. He spent the time going back to review his other answers, no idea what he was looking for.

"'Question twenty-three. Given F of X equals X squared minus 1, and G of X equals two X, find G of F of X.' Hmmm . . . how do we want to play this?" She talked through the problem and he wrote it down as she went.

"Move your hand, I have to see something. Good, you got it. Now cross that answer out."

He stopped writing.

"Seriously. Cross it out. It's all wrong."

The pen didn't move.

"I took the two of X and substituted it into the X squared minus one. That screwed it all up. Don't worry, it was deliberate. If you don't make a few stupid errors you'll look like a genius."

He wrote "RU1" and added a question mark.

She laughed. "No, but I hope to play one in the movies. And what did I say about writing notes? Back to the problem. You solve these things by working backward, so we substitute in X squared minus one for the two X . . ."

Twice during the test Mr. Young walked the aisles. Both times he went past, Sawyer was positive he was busted. And when the kid across from him had a question

143

and Mr. Young squatted down *right there*, his hand on Sawyer's desk for balance, Grace's whisper seemed like a scream. But nothing happened, and Mr. Young went back to his desk and Sawyer's heart went back to beating.

There was forty minutes left when they got to the last question. Sawyer kept his eyes fixed on the equation and waited for Grace to work her magic.

After five minutes he was still waiting, then Grace said, "Sorry. Had to   bathroom break   what   I miss?"

Sawyer wrote a zero on the scrap paper.

"Good plenty time   go back to   with antiderivative after   last   -estion   log 6   squar- minus   plus four equal   -kay   -ing to the zer-   four X   equa-   -us -ositi- "

Then nothing.

No static, no clicks, no buzzing.

Nothing.

Sawyer tapped the frame up by the hinge. He assumed it wouldn't help, and it didn't, but he couldn't think of anything else to do. He took the glasses off, folded them closed, and put them in his shirt pocket, wire-end down, then he stretched and rolled his neck, working out the kinks, rubbing the fuzziness out of his eyes.

He was on his own now.

A half hour and one question to go.

How hard could it be?

Thirty minutes and two sheets of scrap paper later, Sawyer picked a number between one and a hundred and wrote it down.

CHAPTER

20

"**WHO WAS THAT** girl you were with at Starbucks?"

Great.

He couldn't say he wasn't there because obviously somebody saw him. It couldn't have been Zoë, because if she saw him at a Starbucks talking to a girl she didn't know, she would have come in and introduced herself.

Or something like that.

She knew he was at Starbucks and she knew he had been talking to a girl and if he tried to pretend he wasn't he'd only make it worse.

And he couldn't try to joke his way out of it with a *Which Starbucks?* or a *Which girl?* as if he was always bumping into strange girls at Starbucks all over town and couldn't be expected to keep them straight.

They both knew him better than that.

Nope, somebody had seen him and of course that somebody had to let Zoë know, and now there was no way out of it, he had to admit he'd been there and that he had talked to a girl, the crime of the century exposed.

"It was Francis's granddaughter."

There was no way out of it, but it didn't have to be the truth.

"Who's Francis?"

"The guy I work with."

"The one that taught at Harvard? The old guy?"

"Yeah, him. And it was Notre Dame."

A pause. "So how do you know her?"

"I don't. She stopped by his house when I was there yesterday."

"What were you talking about?"

"Nothing. Just hello and stuff."

A longer pause. "What did she give you?"

She knew about that, too. Well, what *did* she give him? There were a lot of ways he could have answered that—hope, friendship, a guilty conscience—but he kept it simple and close to the truth.

"A pair of the old guy's glasses. He left them at her mother's house last night. She wanted me to give them to him at work."

Close enough.

"Why didn't she drop them off?"

"I don't know. I didn't ask."

He kept his eyes on the road, flipping down the visor to block the late afternoon sun. He could tell by the silence that she was going over it in her head, weighing the evidence. Later she'd check his phone, look for any numbers that weren't familiar, but she wouldn't find any since he took care of that.

"Are those the glasses you wore in math?"

Spies everywhere.

"Yeah. My eyes hurt. I was up all night, cramming for the test."

"So you wore somebody else's glasses? That's stupid."

"They're reading glasses. All they do is magnify stuff."

"Did they help?"

He laughed. "Yeah, they did."

"You think you passed?"

"I think I aced it."

Now she laughed.

"Seriously. It was like there was a voice in my head, telling me the answers."

"And you think it was the glasses? Really? That *is* stupid."

"I get the test back Monday. We'll see then."

She held out a minute, maybe even two, before she had to ask. "What's her name?"

"Whose name?"

"That girl, the one at Starbucks."

"Grace McGillicutty."

She smiled. "I thought you said it was her *mother's* father. Her last name wouldn't be McGillicutty."

"Okay, so it's not. It was just a guess."

"But her first name is Grace."

"Yeah. Grace."

She put on the radio, changed it to the channel she liked, then waited until they were driving past Mike's Ice Cream before she said, "Isn't that the same girl that applied for the job?"

He remembered what he had said.

"Yeah. That's the one."

"Did she get it?"

"No."

"Good."

He gave her a look. Two could play that game. "What difference does it make?"

"Do you want to spend your day with some Westie girl? Sandra said that she was a total loser, remember? And Sandra knows some *real* freaks, so that should tell you something."

He thought about saying that Sandra didn't know Grace but that Sandra knew *her*, but it wasn't worth the effort so he let it drop. She didn't say anything after that either, too busy texting.

They were almost to her house when a light went on. She looked over at him, grinning like a cat.

"You don't drink coffee."

That was it.

"You don't like *any* hot drinks."

The one little slipup.

"And they don't sell Mountain Dew."

Busted.

"So what were you doing at Starbucks?"

Think.

Some kind of fruit juice?

No, they had it at school and it was a lot cheaper.

A doughnut?

Yeah, for sure, and they had them at Starbucks, but not the kind he liked, and she knew it.

Think. What would Grace say? What would be her Plan B?

"I wanted to buy a gift card for Mr. Young, give it to him before the test. You know how he loves his frappuccinos."

Her eyes went wide, her mouth dropped open, and he knew he was safe. *"You bribed Mr. Young?"*

He shrugged. "I was going to, yeah. But they wanted twenty bucks for a gift card and I thought that was overdoing it."

"Overdoing it? What are you, crazy? You can't bribe a teacher like that."

"It's not really a bribe. It's more of a joke. I figured it would put him in a good mood when he graded my test."

"That's a bribe, you idiot." She rubbed her temples with her fingertips. "I can't believe it. What were you thinking?"

"Relax. I didn't give him anything."

"But you were *going* to. And Mr. Young? I mean, *my god*, he would have had you suspended in a second. He doesn't joke around about that stuff."

"Well, I didn't—"

"And what would that say about me? Did you think about *that*? How would that make *me* look?"

"Why would it have anything to do with you?"

"Because I go *out* with you. You do something stupid, I look stupid."

"But I didn't do anything."

Zoë sighed. "Sometimes I wonder why I go out with you."

He used to wonder about that too.

The very first time she told him to ask her out, he wondered why.

She was hot.

He was average.

She was popular. Maybe not A-list popular, but popular enough.

He wouldn't have been on any list if it weren't for her.

She had lots of friends. Friends that let her decide where they went and what they did and who was cool and who wasn't worth their time.

He used to have friends.

She could have had her choice of guys, but she went out with him.

And he knew why.

He was safe. With him, she got to set all the boundaries and decide how far they'd get pushed, if they got pushed at all, knowing that he wouldn't even think of challenging them.

He was predictable.

Harmless.

Vanilla.

Boring.

No, not boring.

Obedient.

Fetch. Sit. Roll over. Beg. Stay. He was well trained and housebroken too.

She didn't want a boyfriend.

She wanted a purse poodle.

An accessory.

That's why she went out with him.

But that was okay.

He could have found another girlfriend, maybe, but he went out with her.

And he knew why.

It was easy. Go along to get along, give her what she wanted and he'd get something out of it too. Not always and not often, but enough to keep him around. When she was happy she could be cute and fun, even considerate, and all he had to do to keep her happy was do what she wanted to do. It saved him from ever having to think about it. Wasn't that the way it was supposed to be? Plus his parents liked her. His mom loved when she came over to watch movies, and his dad thought it was great that she baked him cookies from scratch. They had no problem with Zoë being there when they weren't home, and if they assumed they were having sex, they knew Zoë would make sure it stayed safe.

It was easy. That's why he went out with her.

That, and she was hot.

CHAPTER
21

HE SHOULD HAVE called her as soon as the test was over.

It would have taken two seconds—*Hey, thanks a lot, I owe ya*—that sort of thing. But it was a B day and on B days there was only four minutes between classes and if he was late there was a chance he'd be sent to the VP's office for a pass. It had happened once already this year and he doubted it would happen then, but he didn't want to risk it, not with those glasses in his backpack. With his luck Ms. Owens would somehow find out about them, and nothing good would come from that. So he didn't call between classes.

He could have called during lunch, plenty of time

then, but he had to get his economics homework done, ten short-answer questions about a reading he hadn't read. After that it was more classes, then meeting up with Zoë by her locker and that fun ride to her house. Driving home from Zoë's he had the music up so loud he couldn't think about anything, and by the time he pulled into his driveway the events of the morning were pushed so far back into his head they might as well have happened weeks ago. But when his phone started buzzing at eleven that night, he remembered it all.

"Tell me, Mr. Bond, anything interesting happen at school today?"

"Hey, sorry, I meant to call you but—"

"You wouldn't have gotten me anyway. My phone was confiscated."

"What?"

"Tell me about it. The guy that runs detention has a real Napoleon complex. He sees your phone, it's gone."

"Oh. I thought you meant the police."

"That would be better. At least I'd get due process. With this guy I may never see it again."

Sawyer thought for a second. "If they took your phone, how are you—"

"They took *a* phone. You think I let them get the real one? Please."

"Can they do that, just take your phone and not give it back?"

"It's Westside, Mr. Bond. Things are done differently over here."

"What did you get detention for?"

"This crazy rule they have. You can't stroll into school several hours late without a valid reason. Hanging out at Starbucks *is* a reason, but apparently not a valid one."

Damn.

He should have known that.

If he had school, she would have had it too, but he didn't even think to ask, didn't think about the risk on her end at all, only worried about himself. He thought about it now though, and didn't like how it felt.

"Anyway," she said, "what'd you think of the test?"

"I don't know, I didn't take it. What did *you* think of it?"

"Tough. Borderline unfair. The average grade's going to be a C-minus."

"How do you know?"

"Because I know math teachers. The test results will bell-curve out, nice and neat. But there'll be more Fs than As. Especially with those last six questions. Those were cruel."

He had to ask. "How do you think we did?"

"*We?* Cute."

"You know what I meant."

"We did excellent. As long as you wrote it right."

"How'd you get so good at this stuff, anyway? Are you like a math genius or something?"

"No, no genius. They used to call me a child prodigy but then they downgraded me to advanced. I'm a long way from genius."

"Closer than me."

"True. But only in math. And it's probably best if you don't challenge me in chess. Or poker."

"Well, I think you're a genius. You made those glasses."

"All I did was kit-bash some parts together, but thank you for noticing. The best part, though, was the plan. *That* was genius."

"You mapped it all out?"

"Of course."

"What was the code name?"

"Operation Newton Leibniz."

"Who was that?"

"It's who were *they*. Isaac Newton and Gottfried

Leibniz. The fathers of calculus. Who are probably spinning in their graves right now."

"Was it fun?"

"If it wasn't fun—"

"You wouldn't do it," he said, and when he said it she laughed, and hearing her laugh made him smile. The first time all day. "Seriously, Grace. I owe you big-time."

"Glad to hear you say that. Because I need some help with my career project."

Oh crap. He'd forgotten all about it and it was due in what, two weeks, maybe less? He had the damn notes—the notes his father had to look over and correct, plus the notes his mother brought home from her office—but he hadn't started writing it yet, and he knew both his parents would want to see it before he handed it in, and, bet on it, they'd have "revisions" he'd have to make. Still, it was only Thursday. Plenty of time to get it done.

"Hello, Mr. Bond? You there?"

"Sorry. I was thinking about my career project."

"I would have thought you'd have it done by now. I mean, given the risks involved . . ."

"Funny."

"I gotta get mine done too," Grace said. "And I need your help."

"*My* help? Wow, you are desperate."

"No, not desperate. Determined."

"I'm your man. What do you want to be? A professional snake charmer? Cosmonaut? Or are you still thinking underwater welder?"

"The research is all done and I can do the writing no problem. It's another kind of favor."

He hesitated half a second, then said, "Sure. What do you need?"

"Just a ride to the library."

CHAPTER

22

FRIDAY WAS A good day.

It was a C day, which meant they were back to forty-five-minute classes, the so-called "short day" in the rotating, flip-flopping, ass-backward schedule that existed only to complicate their lives. Every fourth C day he had study hall first period, and that meant he could sleep an extra hour, signing himself in just before the next bell. It had taken him until October to convince his parents that missing an occasional study hall wouldn't lead to him flunking out. His mother still called from her job to make sure he was awake and getting ready for school, that he packed a snack and had a few dollars in his wallet. That morning he decided to be up and out before the call came.

It was also the Friday before the start of the Thanksgiving week. Half the school would be out Monday and Tuesday, and nobody—including teachers—felt like doing anything that was going to be graded. He watched an episode of *Más Sabe El Diablo* in Spanish, the last forty minutes of *Saving Private Ryan* in history, and nodded off during a documentary on the International Monetary Fund in economics.

In precalc Mr. Young showed *Graphville*.

Again.

The first time he saw it, Sawyer liked the movie. That was in eighth grade. And he still liked it the two times he saw it freshman year. It was back again in tenth grade, in both art and computer science, but by then it had crossed over from tolerable to painful. Last year his English teacher had them watch it because it was a good example of "metanarrative." Sawyer felt it was also a good example of metatorture. Mr. Young showed it the first week of class. Sawyer didn't mind since he assumed that, as a senior, it would be the last time he'd have to endure it, but on that Friday before Thanksgiving week, when he saw the plastic case in

Mr. Young's hand, Sawyer knew he'd never get out of *Graphville*.

Mr. Young called himself an "early adapter," which was code for geek. He synced the DVD player through the THX surround-sound stereo, showing the movie on the SMART board, providing the class with a "true theater experience," as if somehow that would make it enjoyable. Mr. Young said the setup was "über-tech" and "seamless," and explained to the class how the "dual USB port served as a multicomponent interface." Sawyer was not impressed. He'd seen Grace do better with an old pair of glasses, some hacked electronic parts, and a roll of black tape.

He had expected to feel guilty about cheating and was surprised when he didn't. Grace was right, pre-calculus was just a hoop he was expected to jump, and once through the hoop, he'd never need it again. Getting *around* the hoop was even better. If he kept the grade up for the rest of the quarter—Grace would have a plan for that—he'd have a decent semester average, and that'd be all he'd need to apply to other schools. Thinking about those glasses and that test and how he pulled it off and how he'd do it again had him smiling through *Graphville*.

The cafeteria had pizza for lunch. It was about as good as a day at school was going to get.

Zoë had a good day too, everything back to normal, his Starbucks misadventure forgiven or forgotten or tucked away to be pulled out the next time he did something she thought was stupid. They even fooled around a little before he drove her to work. He spent the night online in the basement rec room, playing *Black Ops* against strangers. Zoë called for a ride home at eleven, and by midnight he was back online for another game. It was close to one when his phone rang.

"You busy?"

"Grace, it's one o'clock in the morning."

"Nope, not quite. You're six minutes fast."

"Whatever."

"So you busy?"

"No. Yes. It's late and—"

"I get it. You've got company."

"*What?* No."

"Oh? Too bad for you. So listen, about that favor you owe me—"

"Can't we talk about this later?"

"Okay. I'll call you back in an hour."

"No, I mean like tomorrow. Afternoon."

"That won't work."

"How come?"

"Because I'm asking now."

"Okay, okay. What is it?"

"I need a lift to the library."

"Grace, you asked me that yesterday, remember? I said I would."

"Good. I want to go to the one we went to before. The one in the house. Okay?"

"You had to call at one o'clock to ask me that?"

"I did. What do you say?"

"Fine, I'll give you a ride. I gotta work at noon so I can pick you up before that or—"

"No."

"No? You just said—"

"I need to go now."

It took a few seconds to sink in.

"You're not stealing that painting."

"Please. Did I say anything about a painting? All I asked for was a ride to the library."

"Yeah, right. Why else would you want to go there now?"

"Maybe I have a book I want to return."

"I'm not driving you."

The line went quiet and he thought that she had hung up, but then she sighed and said what he hoped she wouldn't say.

"I helped you out. You said you owed me one. This is the one I want."

"It's not the same."

"Really? Why?"

"Because it's not. The test, that was just school stuff. It wasn't breaking the law."

"Actually, I think it was."

"Well, I'm not doing it, so it really doesn't matter what it is."

"I don't *want* you there. I just want a ride, that's all. And if you don't drive me, I'll get there on my own."

"How? You don't have a car."

"I'll hitch. I'm halfway there anyway."

"Are you crazy? You can't be hitchhiking. You'll get picked up by some psycho."

"Don't worry about it. I hitch all the time and I've only been killed twice. I'll stop by the ice cream place tomorrow and tell you how it went."

"Wait a second, will you?" He set the phone down and rubbed his face with both his hands, drawing in a

166

long, deep breath that he let out slowly. She'd do it, she'd hitchhike all the way out there. Or at least she'd try. And he'd spend the night worrying about her, imagining every sick thing that could happen—that *would* happen—if he didn't do something. She had to be kidding about the rest, the breaking in and all that, but hitchhiking in the middle of the night, that was something he could see her doing, if only to say she'd done it. He looked at the digital clock on the cable box. 12:57. Damn. This was stupid.

"Where are you now?"

CHAPTER

23

EVERYBODY KNEW SINGH'S Diner. It was down-town, across from the bus station, with a neon sign that said GREAT FO D!, an ancient lunch counter, and wobbly, vinyl-topped stools that were bolted to the floor. He'd been there once, after the junior prom, the limo pull-ing up out front. Hot dogs and fries at sunrise in tie-less tuxes and wrinkled gowns, a slumming adventure they had talked about for months.

Getting out of the house was easier than he thought it would be. He probably could have done it without his parents ever finding out, cutting through the garage and letting the car roll into the street before starting it up, but there was always the chance that on a late night bath-room visit, one of them would notice his car was missing and then the phone calls would start and they would be waiting for him when he got home and that would be it for months. Instead, he knocked on their bedroom door and asked permission. Technically it was permission to go to St. Mary's to help unload a truck of surplus food that had arrived six hours early, a story that rolled off his tongue with surprising ease, but the way Sawyer saw it, St. Mary's was a small detail that was open to last-second change. He knew he should feel bad about lying to his parents—they had always trusted him and he had never given them any reason not to—but as he drove by Singh's, looking for a place to park, it just felt good to be out of the house.

It was a cold night, dark even with the streetlights. At the intersection a black guy in a winter parka nodded from the sidewalk and another motioned for him to roll down his window. Sawyer pretended he didn't see them, staring at the red light and willing it green. He could hear them saying something, laughing as they said it, and when the passenger door flew open he jumped.

"Geez, you went right by me," Grace said, tossing her backpack on the floor and sliding in. "My friends tried to tell you, but you ignored them." She smiled and waved toward the sidewalk, and Sawyer turned and gave a wave too, the guy in the parka laughing louder as he waved back.

"Damn. I should have asked if you wanted me to grab you anything from Singh's. Sorry. We can go back if you want."

"No, it's good," Sawyer said. "I wanna get this over with."

"Tell me about it. This is *so* exciting." She clapped her hands and rubbed them together.

"No gloves?"

"In the bag. Check out my outfit." She took off her purple jacket and flicked on the dome light so he could see her black turtleneck sweater, tight black jeans, and black Doc Martens. She tugged down the front of her black beret and struck a pose. "How do I look?"

"Guilty."

"My ears are freezing but I love this hat so it's worth it." She pulled a SpongeBob folder from her backpack. "I'm calling it Operation Camel Ride. Wanna see the plans?"

"Not really," he said.

"Oh, don't be like that. You're just dropping me off, that's all."

"Won't you need a ride back?"

"You're right. Thanks."

"It wasn't an offer."

"Too late. Besides, I'm only going to be five minutes, tops. Check it out." She unfolded a hand-drawn map and laid it across her lap. "The parking lot, the Dumpster, the main entrance, the handicap ramp, there's a door here and here and a fire door over here. These are all windows. And this is the room with the painting. You can drop me off down the road, right about here. It'll be really dark since there are no streetlights."

"How do you know?"

"Google Maps. Street view. Saved me a lot of time."

"I'm sure they'd be happy to know that."

"This is a church next door. Lots of bushes in front. There's a sign with a light on it, but it's way over here. Shouldn't be a problem. I go like this," she traced a dotted line with her finger around the side of the church to the back of the library, "go in here, up the back stairs, down the hall, into the room, grab the painting, check to make sure the coast is clear, then out the front door, across the street to the park, past the swings and the basketball court to this side street here where you'll be waiting. Easy."

"How you gonna get in, pick the lock?"

She took a wire coat hanger from her bag, twisted the hook, and it sprung free, then straightened out the bends. "They have a crash bar on the back door, you know the type? It's the same as the one at my aunt's apartment building, and they're the old style so there's a nice size gap between the doors. You push the hook end in, wiggle it around so you catch the bar, then give it a yank. It took me months to learn how to do it, but now it's no problem."

"What do you do when the alarm goes off?"

She held up a paper from the folder. "Found this online. Minutes of the Friends of the Wood Library meeting in October. The highlighted part."

"I'm driving. Just read it to me."

"Okay . . . 'The finance committee's report included a request for additional funds to repair the crown cornice that was damaged by the August fourth lightning strike.' And then a little bit further on it says '. . . funds would also be allocated to update the library's alarm system that was rendered inoperative.' There *is* no alarm."

"And if there is?"

"I run. I'm not stupid."

He thought about arguing the point, but that would just make her mad. Instead he said, "You know you can't do this, right?"

She looked at her map. "Which part?"

"The whole thing. You can't go stealing things you want. It's wrong."

"I'm not stealing it, remember? I'm borrowing it for a few days. I'm bringing it back."

"Is that what you'll tell them if you get caught: you were only borrowing it?"

"I've got a plan. I'm not getting caught."

"But what if you do? Then what happens?"

She paused, then smiled. "I get it. You think that I'd tell them about you."

That's what he was thinking, but he said, "No, I wasn't thinking that."

"Yes, you were. But don't worry, I would never rat you out. That's not my style. Besides, I wouldn't want to share the credit."

That was the truth. And somehow he knew it. She'd never tell.

"What if they stop us while we're driving away?"

"You had no idea what I was doing. You were just giving me a ride."

"They wouldn't believe that I'd drive you all the way out here for nothing."

"Sure they would. I'll say that I promised to have

sex with you if you did. That's the kind of thing they'll believe. But don't *you* go getting any ideas."

He laughed at that. She was right, it was the kind of thing a guy would do. She refolded her map, put the map in the folder, put the folder in the bag, and pulled the zippers tight. She checked her mini flashlight, then worked on the coat hanger. He glanced over to see her face.

"You nervous?"

She smiled. "Excited. And a little nervous, I guess. But it's a good nervous. You?"

He was about to say he was scared shitless, but then he realized that that wasn't true. He should've been nervous—no, *terrified*—but he wasn't.

He felt something, yeah, but what?

He had felt this way before, but it had never been so intense, so electrifying.

Stop.

It was wrong. And illegal. And he should turn around, drop her off somewhere, and never think about Grace again. Let her go get famous on her own, let him get on with his life.

And that's when it first came to him. Not the whole thing, just a hint of it, a whisper.

This wasn't about Grace.

It wasn't about giving her a ride so she wouldn't hitch-hike, and it wasn't about keeping her safe, although he did like the way that sounded.

And it wasn't about paying back a debt, either. He owed a bigger one to his parents and was willing to let that go.

This was about something else, something he felt when he was making that bet with his father. He felt it wearing those glasses for the test and when he was balancing the painting on his knees. There was a word for it, there had to be, but it wouldn't come to him, not yet, anyway. But he knew it wasn't about Grace.

It was about him.

He cracked open the window and took a deep breath of ice-cold air. His heart pounded in his chest—strong, steady, a little faster but not much.

"I'm probably not as nervous as you. You've got the hard part, I'm just driving."

"Sorry. Can't change the plan now. This is a one-woman job."

"That's fine by me," he said. Then he asked something he'd been wondering about since she called.

"How'd you get out of the house?"

"I walked out, what do you think?"

"I mean what did you tell your parents? Won't they wonder where you were all night?"

Even in the dim light he could see her expression change. "What are you getting at?"

"I'm not getting at anything. I only asked what you told your parents."

"Do *I* ask *you* questions like that?"

"I don't know, maybe."

"Well, I don't."

"It's just that you know a lot about me and all I know about you is—"

"What difference does it make?"

"It doesn't make *any* difference."

"Then stop prying and leave it that way."

"I'm not prying. I'm being friendly."

She looked over at him. "I thought we were friends."

"We are, but—"

"Friends aren't *friendly*, they're just friends. Friendly's what you are with people who *aren't* your friends. And if you're my friend, you'll drop it," she said, and then in a softer voice, "okay?"

Sawyer nodded but didn't say anything, and it got quiet for a few miles.

Grace said, "It's a good plan."

"It is."

"How'd you like the map?"

"Very detailed."

"How about that research on the alarm?"

"That was impressive."

"Thanks."

"I like that coat-hanger trick."

"I'll show you how to do it next time you come over to my aunt's place. You never know when it'll come in handy."

"Got a movie picked out?"

"*The Asphalt Jungle.* 1950. Directed by John Huston."

"Black-and-white?"

"Of course," she said, and it got quiet again. Five minutes later she said, "Now, you ready for this?"

He clicked on the directional for the off ramp.

CHAPTER 24

THE SECOND TIME the cop car drove by, Sawyer was sure they had her.

He was parked on the side street. Across the open space, through the jungle gym and between the trees, he could see the front of the library. And thanks to the floodlight in the parking lot—the one she didn't plan for—he and anybody else who cared to look could see the tall white doors. He had thought he had seen one of them open a bit before the cop car drove by, but they were shut now and there was still no sign of Grace.

It was easy to imagine her handcuffed, sitting in the back of a patrol car, the cop pulling the painting out of her black bag as he called it in to the station. And it was easy to imagine things getting a lot worse after that.

The plan wasn't working.

She had been right about the church. It was dark and there were plenty of bushes to hide behind, but as they had come down the road, they could see that there were lights Google Maps didn't show.

"Looks like there's a floodlight over the back door. I don't think you can see it from the street. I won't know till I get there."

"There's one in front, too. And there's one pointing up the flagpole."

"I can avoid those. I think we'll be okay."

"What about the front doors?"

"I'll only be in the light for a few seconds. Shouldn't be a problem."

He had looked over at her, no expression. "You still want to do this?"

She had yanked on her gloves and pointed to a clump of bushes near the sidewalk. "If I'm not at the meeting point in fifteen minutes, go home."

He had pulled over and she had slipped out, then he pulled away as she disappeared into the darkness.

That was thirty-eight minutes ago.

The cop car went past the library—it might have slowed down a bit, he couldn't tell—and continued on toward the Dollar General. Sawyer knew it was exactly three point one miles down the road. That was in her plan. Drop her off, drive three point one miles to the store, turn around in the parking lot, drive back, turn right at the stop sign, take the first left, then left onto the street that ran along the side of the park, wait for her there near the sign that said NO SKATEBOARDING. Keep to the speed limit and it would take nine minutes. It took him twelve.

The park was at the center of the village. A mile in any direction and you were in farmland. You'd have to get back on the expressway and drive north ten miles to hit the outer suburbs, another ten to be back in the city. There were some homes in this part of the village, big old houses like the one they had turned into the library, and a few empty storefronts on the main road. He was parked across the street from a gas station that had FOR SALE painted on the sheet of plywood that covered the window. Next to that was an open lot stacked with tires. She had been right about one thing: there were no street-lights and, other than the front of the library, it was dark.

He looked across the park. Nothing.

Forty minutes.

He checked his rearview mirrors, no one sneaking up from behind. Too dark to see them if they were.

Movement.

A small black shape dropping off the side of the library stairs, away from the light.

Then nothing.

Fifty minutes.

It was probably his imagination.

Maybe just some shadow.

Some leaves blowing across the steps, an old newspaper caught in the wind—then the car door popping open, slamming shut, Grace saying "Go, go, go," strapping on her seatbelt as the police car slowly rounded the corner and started down the street toward them.

They turned and looked at each other.

"Not good," she said.

The headlights rolled closer.

"I didn't plan for this."

Half a block away, the lights slowed.

"I—I don't know what to do."

"I do," he said, and he leaned in and put his arm around

her shoulder, flipping her arm around his. "Kiss me."

"*What?* No way—"

"Shut up and kiss me," he said, drawing her in, pressing his lips against hers, keeping one eye on the approaching lights.

Zoë wasn't the first girl he had ever kissed, but he hadn't kissed any other since tenth grade. And now Grace. Her face was cold, her lips chapped, and they didn't taste like strawberry or peaches the way Zoë's lips did. It was an awkward kiss, unfamiliar and strange, but when he heard the cop car drive up, pause, then drive on, he knew he'd never forget it.

"He's gone," he said, pulling away enough to look at the passenger side rearview.

She leaned back in her seat, eyes wide. "Oh my god," she said, "that was brilliant," and pulled him in for a second kiss, this one fast and on the cheek. "I didn't know what to do. I didn't plan on *anything* like that. You're a genius."

He sat up and started the car and pulled away from the curb.

"I can't believe it. *How* did you know to do that?"

"Let's just say I've been in that situation before."

She laughed louder than he had ever heard her laugh. And he laughed too, his hands not shaking enough to notice. He glanced over to the black bag on the floor.

It was too dark to tell, but he knew she was smiling.

CHAPTER
25

IT WAS COLD and windy and miserable and it was snowing that wet, slushy snow that came down like slow, fat rain.

It was not ice cream weather.

But since noon there had been a steady stream of customers who—god knows why—had to have an ice cream, and it was after two before Sawyer was able to take a break. He didn't mind that it was busy. The time went by fast, and it kept him from thinking about what he had done twelve hours before.

He leaned against the counter, facing the street, and that's when he noticed the cop climbing out of the police car.

Behind him, the freezer door slammed shut.

"Looks like you're in trouble, Sawyer," Francis McGillicutty said.

"Maybe."

The cop zippered up her jacket and adjusted her hat.

"It's not your fault, but you can bet you'll catch hell for it."

"Uh-huh."

She stepped up on the sidewalk and started toward the door.

"Nothing to do but tell 'em the truth."

"Yeah."

"Just tell 'em. Say sorry, but we're all out of Rocky Road. They'll just have to make due with Fudge Ripple."

And she walked past without even looking in.

Sawyer took a deep breath and let it out slow and choppy. "What are you talking about, Francis?"

"John and Cassandra."

"Who?"

"The *Bordens*. They're going to be here anytime now. And you know how they love their Rocky Road."

"I'm sure I can handle it."

"Hope so, for your sake. You know the Bordens."

He didn't, but he nodded anyway.

"Look at the time. I was supposed to clock out at two

and here it is almost twenty after and I'm still hanging around. Can you believe it?"

He could believe it.

"I suppose I could stay if you think you'll need help."

"I'll be fine, thanks."

Francis swapped his apron for his winter coat and was about to leave when the bells on the front door rang and she walked in. They both looked at her and she smiled back.

Oh boy.

"Want me to get this one?"

No, get the hell out of here, Sawyer thought, but it was too late, she was already at the counter.

"Wow, it's *soooo* cold out there," she said, then looked at the old man. "Francis, right? I'm Zoë. Sawyer's girl-friend. I've heard about you."

Go. Please go.

"Really? I hope he made me sound better than I am."

"I think being a professor at Notre Dame is pretty good."

Leave. Now.

"A professor at *Notre Dame*? That would be very good. Good luck with that."

"Oh, I don't want to be—"

"Hey, hon, how about some ice cream? See you later, Francis."

"Ice cream? Hello? Didn't I say I was freezing?"

"Sawyer, if you'd like, I could brew up a pot of coffee—"

"*No*. I mean, thanks, Francis, but don't bother. And Zoë, uh, you *sure* you don't want an ice cream? We have mint chocolate-chip? My treat? Good-bye, Francis."

Francis grinned and winked at Sawyer. "I hear ya. Nice to meet you, miss."

"Nice to meet you too," she said, and he was *this* close to being out of the store when she said, "Oh, and thanks for helping Sawyer out, you know, with the math test."

She had her back to Sawyer, so when he made a just-humor-her face, she didn't see it. But Francis did and picked up on it and left without saying anything, which was very cool for an old guy.

Zoë started in right away, declaring Francis weird and deciding that a mint chocolate-chip ice cream sounded good after all. She made a show of licking the cone from end to end before dropping the act and just eating it, telling him how she was going out to dinner with her family that night, how she was going to get the shrimp scampi and those little buttered potatoes, when the bells on the door jangled again and Grace walked in.

Perfect.

Sawyer watched as she unzipped her purple jacket, unwrapped her red scarf, took off her black beret, and ran a hand through her hair. He should have told Grace about the whole Starbucks thing and how Francis was her grandfather and how she really wanted a job at Mike's Ice Cream, but he hadn't, so he said, "You just missed him."

And instead of saying thanks and heading back out, instead of pretending she didn't see him waving his hands behind Zoë's back like he was landing a jet, pointing to the door and mouthing *Go*, Grace walked to the counter and said, "Missed who?"

"Your grandfather. He just left," Sawyer said, and when he saw Zoë's eyes go wide, he knew he had said the wrong thing.

Zoë turned and stared at Grace, her smile curling into a dismissive smirk as Sawyer read her mind. *So this is Grace.*

"My grandfather? Really?" Grace stepped around Zoë to look in the cooler. "What was he doing here?"

Zoë looked at Sawyer and rolled her eyes while he

closed his. Zoë said, "Doesn't he *work* here?"

"Nope," Grace said, then looked up at Sawyer and smiled. "Not on Saturdays, anyway."

"He usually works weekdays. He was covering for, uh, Juan. If he comes back I'll tell him you were here."

Grace looked at Zoë's ice cream and Zoë glared back, so of course Grace had to say something. "What'ja get?"

"Mint chocolate-chip," Zoë said, the words sounding a lot like *None of your damn business.*

"Got any coffee ice cream? I was up all night and could use the caffeine."

Another eye roll from Zoë.

Grace went for a medium sugar cone with Oreo pieces, and as he punched the numbers into the cash register he heard Grace say, "Did you guys hear about the painting somebody stole last night?"

Zoë was ignoring her and he wasn't going to say a thing, but that didn't stop Grace.

"Seriously. Somebody broke into the Wood Library last night. Took a painting *right off the wall*. Police haven't got a *clue.*"

"Fifteen twenty-three's your change. Thanks. Good-bye."

"*Apparently* it's a Post-Impressionist oil painting done

189

in a loose *Orientalist* style by an artist named Ravlin. It could be worth *millions*."

Sawyer bent down to pick up the rack of ice cream scoops he had knocked over, and on his knees he prayed she'd be gone when he stood.

"It's not big, either. It'd fit in my backpack, easy."

"*Hey*, uh, Grace? Yeah, Grace, right. I'll ah, I'll tell your grandfather you were here. So long."

That smile, then a wink only he could see. She zipped up her coat and pulled on her beret, careful not to drop her cone, and headed for the door. "If he stops back, tell him I've got the movie he wanted to see." She tapped a finger along the side of her nose and left, waving as she passed the window.

"She's a freak," Zoë said.

"She's definitely something," Sawyer said as he watched her disappear down the street.

CHAPTER

26

TEN MINUTES AFTER his shift was supposed to be over, his replacement strolled in. It was the owner's nephew, and he showed up, as usual, late, stoned, and smelling of patchouli oil. He was focused on making himself a chocolate sundae and didn't look up when Sawyer said good-bye.

On the drive home, Sawyer had time to think.

There had been a few problems—those lights they didn't expect, Grace dropping the coat hanger as she cut through the bushes, the cop car going back and forth past the library a million times—but, just like with the test and the treaty, it went according to her plan. She had waited until they were on the expressway before she showed him the painting. It was hard to see in the car, but he didn't want her to put on the inside light or do anything that would attract attention, like pulling over on the side of the road just to get a peek. She had it now, and if he wanted to see it all he had to do was ask. But if he never saw it again that would be fine too.

She had to be making up that "worth millions" crap. If it were worth anything close to a million it wouldn't have been hanging in the library on the same wall as the *Yo Gabba Gabba!* poster. Somebody would have spotted it and they would have put it in the art museum or sold it off to raise money long ago. It was worth something, sure, but millions? Not likely.

He laughed, remembering how she filled him in, acting it out in the front seat as he drove to the west side, all the sound effects, the facial expressions, the excitement. Maybe that was her talent, telling stories. Maybe that was what would make her famous.

Then there was that kiss.

Didn't see *that* coming.

Sawyer remembered the look in her eyes before she squeezed them shut, how she tensed up and held her breath, how he kept one eye open enough to watch the patrol car roll by. He thought about what he *didn't* do, how he didn't panic or do anything stupid, and how he didn't sit there like a chump, waiting for it all to fall apart. What he did was size up the situation, consider the risks, and take action. Just like that. So what if it wasn't as brilliant as Grace said it was, it was still pretty frickin' cool.

The more he thought about it, the more that kiss meant to him.

When he dropped her off, close to three and a street away from her house, she said something that wouldn't go away.

"Thanks for the best night of my life."

He had thought about that as he drove home, thought about it more as he fell asleep, and it was on his mind when he crawled out of bed the next morning. And he thought about it now as he pulled into his driveway.

The best night of her life.

What did that say about her life?

And if he felt the same way, what did it say about his?

His phone rang and he flipped it open and the screaming started.

"OHMYGODOHMYGODOHMYGOD-
OHMYGODOHMYGODOHMYGOD! I'M GOING
TO *ARUUUUBAAAAAA!*"

He held the phone away from his ear and checked the number, not that he had to. It was Zoë, and apparently her father had surprised her by announcing he was taking the family to Aruba for Thanksgiving. Last year he had surprised her by taking the family to St. Thomas, and the year before the surprise was a cruise. When she was a freshman and her older sister was a senior, they went to the Sandals Resort in Jamaica, but that wasn't a surprise since Zoë got to pick it. And now she was going to Aruba. What a surprise.

"*Oh my god*, Sawyer, guess what my daddy just did?"

Daddy?

He guessed and she screamed some more and he waited.

"I can't *believe* it! This is *so* out of the blue! I mean, I was planning on Thanksgiving here, you know, just my family, and then—oh my god! Aruba! Can you *believe* it?"

She told him that they were leaving in the morning and that she had nothing—absolutely *nothing*—to wear, and that she and her mom were going straight to the mall and then she'd be up all night packing because they were flying out at, like, seven and that meant they'd have to be at the airport at, like, five or something and what was she going to pack and this was so exciting and soooo unexpected and, oh yeah, she wouldn't be able to see him that night but he understood, right? because he was so amazing, and oh my god, Aruba.

He sat in the driveway and listened to it all and said the things she wanted him to say and didn't say the things he knew she didn't want to hear, like how he had been looking forward to spending time with her or that it must be nice to be that rich or to have parents who gave you anything you wanted. He had said those things the last time her father gave her a surprise and it didn't go over well.

There was something else, something he couldn't explain and wouldn't have told her if he could. That feeling he had had last night when he drove Grace to the library, the same one he felt when he thought about the precalc test and the bet. Sure, he wanted to hang out with Zoë. All that time off? They'd end up having *some* kind of sex. But the more he thought about Zoë going away for a week, the stronger that feeling became.

"When I get back I'm going to be *so* tan, and you *know* what that means," she said, lowering her voice and adding a growl. He knew what she meant, that he'd get to check out her tan lines himself, up close. And he also knew it was just part of her act.

"I wish you were going with me," she said, making it sound sincere. "What are you gonna do over break?"

He could have said "nothing" or "study" or "play *Black Ops* online," but he knew he didn't want to do any of those things, that feeling already hinting at adventures he couldn't foresee.

So he told her the truth. "I don't have a plan yet."

"Here's what you're going to do over break," his mother said, dishing a second scoop of mashed potatoes onto his plate. "Number one, finish that career project."

"You're *still* working on that? I can't believe this. Your mother and I have all but written the damn thing for you."

"It's not due until the Monday we get back. I've got plenty of time."

"You *had* plenty of time."

"This is exactly why your father and I wanted you to start early. You do this every quarter, Sawyer, wait till the last second and then rush, rush, rush to get it done."

"You better break that habit soon, son. Once you start at Wembly the work will come at you fast and furious."

"That's *so* true," his mother said. "We'll have to have a set check-in time every night so we can keep on top of your assignments. Your freshman year at college is the most important. You get low grades then, it drags your GPA down for the rest of your degree."

"Yeah. I was thinking about Wembly—"

"You better get thinking about this project or there won't be a Wembly," his father said. "It's a graduation *requirement*. You know what that means?"

"Yes. I know."

"No paper, no diploma."

"I know, Dad. I'll have it done." Sawyer took his time pouring gravy over his potatoes. "I still want to apply to other schools, see what happens."

His father chuckled, shaking his head. "You won't let that drop, will you?"

"It's something I want to do."

"Fine, knock yourself out. And like I said, we'll even pay the registration fees," his father said, pausing for effect. "That is, if you ace your precalculus test."

"I think I did."

"You think you *aced* it?"

"Yeah. I do."

"We're talking an A here, right?"

"Right. An A."

"Great. I hope you did. I mean it, son. You ace that test and I'll be glad to pay your registration fee."

"Fee*s*. I'm looking at a bunch of different schools."

"We'll worry about that when you bring home the A."

Sawyer nodded and started in on the chicken. "I should get the test back Monday."

"*Anyway*, about that project," his mother said. "I want to see a complete first draft Thursday morning before we head to your aunt Paula's for Thanksgiving. And if you're really going to be sending out more applications, you're going to have to get those essays to me next week *at the latest*. If they're anything like the last one, they'll be filled with errors."

More chuckles from his father. "Wait till we see the A."

* * *

He made two calls that night.

The first was to Zoë. She said she was too busy to talk, then talked for forty minutes, the last ten saying the things he could have bet she would say, things like "sorry I won't be around" and "I'll make it up to you when I get back" and "you better be good." There were things he could have said and should have said, but in the end all he said was, "Have a good time."

The second call was to Grace.

CHAPTER 27

THEY MET SUNDAY afternoon at a Dunkin' Donuts on the west side, away from the malls, across the street from the no-name plaza, the one with six empty storefronts, a Radio Shack, and a takeout pizza joint. Not the kind of place Zoë's friends would know about. And Zoë, if her flight left on time, had already been in Aruba long enough to find a hotel bar that would serve a gin and tonic to a seventeen-year-old with a bad fake ID.

Sawyer had a tropical fruit smoothie, Grace had a large black coffee, and they shared a box of doughnut holes. They were the only customers and they sat far from the counter and away from the window.

"Nothing in the paper this morning, nothing online,

nothing on the library's website. I don't even think any-one noticed yet."

"According to you, the police are all over it."

"Consider the source."

"So it's not worth millions?"

"It *could* be."

"So could your coffee."

"The hazelnut maybe, but not regular. The painting's worth more."

"How much more?"

"What difference does it make? I'm bringing it back. Unless you have a better idea."

"No."

"Then I'll bring it back."

"When?"

"They have to realize it's missing first."

"And if they don't?"

"I'll send them a text," she said, smiling to let him know she was kidding.

"You gonna put it back the same way you got it?"

"I'll bring it in during the day. Under my coat or something."

"I suppose you'll need a ride out there when you do."

"Don't know. Haven't planned it yet."

"Oh, that's right, you have to have a *plan*."

"Don't mock my methods. Planning's the best part. Like a giant logic problem."

"Yeah, that's fun all right."

"It can be. Check it out." She held up the last doughnut hole. "This is a rare black diamond." She dropped it in the cardboard box and squeezed the lid shut. "How can I get it without touching the box?"

"Use a fork."

"No forks allowed."

"Okay. Get a couple of straws and—"

"No straws, either. Plastic sets off the alarm."

"You didn't say that before."

"Improvise."

He sipped his drink and thought about it. "What if you wrap a napkin around—"

"That's *still* touching it." She sat up, rubbed her hands together, then held them both out, palms up, and closed her eyes. "Here, let me show you how it's done. It takes skill. Give me the doughnut."

He opened the box, took out the doughnut hole, and placed it in her hand. She opened her eyes and smiled and then it clicked.

"That's a stupid trick," he said.

"Only because you fell for it."

"And it wasn't much of a plan."

"What do you want? It's a doughnut. Give me a better challenge and I'll give you a better plan."

"Like your fun, famous, and rich plan?"

She swirled the coffee in her cup. "You're not having fun?"

He was. A different kind of fun. Not Xbox fun or birthday fun or sex fun. More like hands up, first car in the roller coaster, busted-safety-bar fun. Only better than that.

"I'll give you the fun part," he said. "And I'll give you the fame part, too. I'll call the Crime Stoppers tip line and tell them you stole the painting. That'll make you famous. Fast."

"I think what you mean is *in*famous."

"What's the difference?"

"These days? Nothing. But that's small-*f* fame. I want all-caps fame. In lights. With paparazzi. And my own TV show."

"What about one of those little dogs to put in your purse?"

She waved it off. "That's ancient. I'm getting a monkey."

"Too bad the painting's not worth millions or you'd

203

be rich. Then you'd have all three."

"I'm not worried about the money. If you're famous enough, you don't need it."

"Then you're going to have to steal something *really* big to get that famous. How about the Hope Diamond?"

"I told you, stealing diamonds is next to impossible. If I'm gonna have to steal something to get famous, I'm stealing art."

"Okay. How about the *Mona Lisa*?"

"It's in Paris. And besides, it's been done."

He jabbed his straw into the icy mush at the bottom of his cup and laughed.

"You don't believe me? Look it up."

"It's not that. I'm just wondering if they had to have a code name before they could steal it."

She kicked his foot under the table. "I know when I'm being mocked."

"I'm not mocking. I'm thinking about all the fun you missed out on not being there to plan that one."

"It was a hundred years ago."

"Still, stealing a famous painting from a museum. *That* must have been something to plan," he said, and as soon as he said it, as soon as he saw her eyes go wide and light up in that weird, electric way, he knew it was a mistake.

"Oh. My. God."

A big mistake.

"Do you know how much *fun* that would be?"

"Forget it."

"You'd have to case the joint and draw maps, *lots* of maps . . ."

"The library was one thing—"

"You'd have to plan for the alarms and for the guards . . ." She looked across the table and smiled like he'd never seen her smile before.

"Grace?"

"Tell me," she said, leaning in, "you got any plans for the break?"

CHAPTER

28

SAWYER TOSSED THE half-eaten slice on his plate.

It was Hawaiian, his favorite, and it was from Mark's Pizzeria, the place he liked, but he wasn't hungry anymore.

"A deal's a deal, son," his father said. "And that's not an A."

It wasn't an A.

It was an A+.

After the curve, sure, but that's the grade that went in the book, the highest grade in the class, everybody else ten points behind. A couple of answers at the end of the test were wrong but he got partial credit anyway, Mr. Young saying that the calculations showed he was on the right path and simply slipped up on a few tricky spots.

As for the last answer, well, that wasn't even close.

Still, it was an A+ and he won, only now his father was rewriting the rules, and Sawyer was losing.

"You got an eighty-six point five, correct?"

"Yeah, but—"

"Eighty-six point five. Right here on the school's website it says that an A-minus is ninety to ninety-two, an A is ninety-three to ninety-eight, and an A+ is ninety-eight and above." His father held up his iPhone to show him the proof. "You got an eighty-six point five. That's a solid B, which is a good grade for you."

It was a good grade for him, and Sawyer knew it. But he knew this wasn't about grades anymore, or precalc, or college.

It was about winning.

It was about taking risks, going big, the Hail Mary when the other guy was expecting a punt, jumping through the hoop—no, *around* the damn hoop—and having the balls to pull it off. If it had all fallen apart, if he had gotten caught, he would have had to man up and take the blame. His father would have insisted on it. But it *didn't* fall apart and he *didn't* get caught and now he wanted the credit.

Sawyer picked up the test paper and looked at the

grade, the *Excellent!* written in red ink below the A+ that was a B that might as well have been an F. A month ago he would have sighed and gone with it. Been pissed, yeah, but that was all. Now?

"I'm not going to Wembly."

They laughed.

"Of course you are," his mother said, refilling his glass.

"I told you to stop worrying. You're already in. You got the letter—"

"No. That's not what I meant. I'm not going to go there."

This time they didn't laugh and the room got quiet and he could feel his parents looking at each other, then looking back at him, waiting for him to say he was only kidding, but they were too late. His father plopped down his slice and leaned back in his chair. "When did you decide this?"

"A while ago."

A sigh, a headshake. His mom tagged in.

"What's wrong with Wembly?"

"There's nothing wrong with it. It's just not where I want to go."

"So where *do* you want to go?"

"I'm not sure. I'm still trying to decide what I want to do."

Dad back in. "You can decide while you're at Wembly."

"Wouldn't that be a waste of money?"

Another laugh. "Oh, *now* you're worried about money."

"The counselor said I might be able to get a scholarship to a state school. Not full tuition, but something."

"And what about room and board, what would you do about that? If you're so worried about money, think about what we'd save with you living at home."

"Have you talked about this with Zoë?"

Zoë? "No."

"Don't you think you should?"

He didn't, but he knew what his mother would say if he said that, so he said nothing.

"Maybe what you should do is take some time over Thanksgiving break and *really* think about this. Make a list. Put all the reasons why you should go to Wembly in one column and the reasons to go someplace else in another. That way you'll see why Wembly is the right school for you."

"This whole thing is ridiculous," his father said, picking his slice back up, the pineapple chunks flying off.

"You don't know what you want to be, you don't know where you want to go, and you don't know how you're going to pay for it."

His mother smiled at Sawyer and put her hand on top of his, giving it a little squeeze, balancing the attack. "Sawyer, we understand. Thinking about college is probably the scariest thing you've ever done—"

He had to laugh at that.

"—but your father and I will make sure everything goes smoothly."

"Yeah."

"And remember, we're *always* here for you."

"Oh, I remember."

"And we'll be with you, *every step of the way.*"

"I know."

"We won't be going *anywhere.*"

"Uh-huh."

"And Zoë will be *right* there with you too."

"Yup."

"So really, you have nothing to worry about."

"I guess not."

She gave his hand another squeeze. "You know what you need to do, what would make things a lot easier for you? You need to sit down and draw up a plan."

He looked over at her.

"Trust me," she said, and now she was patting his hand, letting him know it was good advice, "you'll feel better just working on a plan."

She was right. He did feel better when he was working on a plan.

Operation Trick-or-Treat. Operation Newton Leibniz. Operation Camel Ride. All good plans.

So maybe it was time for a few more.

Like Operation Anywhere-But-Wembly and Operation Anything-But-Insurance-Actuary.

He smiled and picked up his pizza, his hunger returning.

CHAPTER 29

"**WHAT DO YOU** think the artist was trying to say?"

Sawyer tilted his head one way, then the other, taking in the wall-sized painting.

"I think he's trying to tell us that there was a sale on blue paint."

Grace nodded. "There *is* a lot of blue."

"That's pretty much all there is."

"According to this, it's called 'Blue Square Number Four' and it's considered one of the most important works in the Color Field movement."

He glanced over at the brochure the woman at the desk had given them when they paid the evening student-rate admission. It had a small picture of the painting, the blue a shade or two off.

"Please tell me you're not thinking this one."

"I don't like paintings that are bigger than me."

"Well, that's going to seriously limit our options."

"Very funny." She flipped to the map at the center of the brochure and took a stubby pencil out from behind her ear. "How many steps was it from the last painting to this one?"

"Seventy-one."

"Do you remember what it was from the front desk to that African mask?"

"Two hundred and fifteen."

She wrote the numbers over the lines she had drawn on the map connecting exit doors to points inside the museum.

"All we've got left to get here is the distance from that statue to the side fire exit and this section's done."

"You still have to pick out a painting."

"I *was* going to go with that one of the woman on the pink elephant. The French one."

"Good choice."

"But did you see how they hang the paintings? They're all flat against the wall."

"Isn't that how they usually do it?"

"Yeah, but it's different here. The one at the library had

a wire on the back and there was a hook on the wall. Like what you'd do at home. Check it out." She stepped up to an empty space on the wall between two paintings. "These have special brackets or something. You can see them when you look from the side."

He leaned in, a dull metal edge just visible at the top and bottom corners.

"Do you lift it off straight or slide it like this *then* lift it off," she said, moving her hands as she said it to show him what she meant. "Or do you have to use some kind of freaky tool to unlock it? I don't know."

"*You* don't know something? That's a first."

"It happens to the best of us. But don't worry, I have a Plan B." She tugged his coat sleeve then led him past the giant blob paintings, through the gallery of dark portraits with carved frames, around the medieval furniture you couldn't sit on, past the Impressionist gallery, past the old book in the glass case, under the swinging metal mobile, to a small hallway where a row of black-and-white photographs were hung an inch off the wall, suspended from the ceiling by thin wires. They were all the same size, about as big as a cafeteria tray, with the same white mat and narrow black frame, and they all showed close-ups of the same woman looking up at tall buildings.

"I saw these the last time I was here. This one's my favorite. There's something familiar about it."

Of course there was. The hat, the short haircut, the weird eyes, the way the corners of the woman's mouth turned up with her smile. No wonder Grace liked it.

"And look, at the end of the hall. A fire exit."

Sawyer nodded, then stepped closer to the photograph, his eyes focused on the wire that ran down behind the frame. "Shouldn't be hard to get through. Regular pair of wire cutters ought to work."

"Already on the shopping list."

"I'd get some wire, too. For practice."

She penciled it in the margin.

"This still a one-person job?" he asked.

"Absolutely," she said, writing.

"Then what I would do is hold the picture against the wall with my head; that way I'd have both hands free to squeeze the wire cutter, just in case it's some titanium wire or something."

Grace smiled. "Nice. I didn't think of that."

"Do you know where this door goes?"

"It says 'fire exit,' so I'm thinking it goes straight outside." She checked the map. "I can't tell looking at this. We'll take the long way around to the parking lot. That way we can be sure."

They walked back to the main gallery and looked around some more, Sawyer re-counting the steps between doorways and corners, Grace writing it all down. When they had what they needed, they sat on a bench in front of a painting of a sailboat setting out in rough seas.

"I put a little X where there's a camera. See? One in every gallery, one in the hall, one near the door. Way high up."

"You saw the guards, right?"

She laughed. "Rent-a-cops. Can you believe it? The museum doesn't even have its own security. And did you see the size of them? They couldn't run ten feet without taking a break. No guns, either, just radios."

He looked at the map. "They must have an office somewhere. Probably over here where it says 'Administration.'"

"Good. That's all the way on the other side of the building."

"If that's where it is, yeah. But it could be anywhere. Would you wait for a shift change or something?"

"Don't be silly. If it's a shift change there'd be twice as many guards here. No, it's got to be at three a.m. exactly."

"Because . . . ?"

"Because that's when late-night workers tend to nod off. Seriously. Lots more accidents at three in the morning than at any other time."

"*Exactly* at three?"

"No, but a good plan has an exact start time, and mine's three a.m."

They sat quietly for a while, Grace checking her map, Sawyer watching the other visitors—all six of them—as they glanced at the artwork, listening to the humming audio tour on their phones. A uniformed guard waddled by, panting as she passed.

For ten minutes they sat like this, then Sawyer said, "Your way won't work."

Grace turned. "Excuse me?"

"What you're thinking. It won't work."

"Oh, really? And how do you know what I'm thinking?"

"The way you're holding the map, with the main entrance at the top. You're thinking of coming in there, past the front desk, around that gallery to the hallway, and then out the fire door."

"It's the fastest route. Count up the steps."

"Maybe. But you're putting yourself that much closer to the security office."

"*If* it's over there. You said so yourself."

"There's a lot of turns. And it'll be dark. You couldn't go as fast. Here, give me that." He took the map and turned it upside down. "There's another entrance over here. It's where they bring in school groups. It's halfway around the back. You can't see it from the road."

"But there's two sets of doors to get through there."

"Yeah, crash-bar doors, just like the ones at the library. Those are your specialty, right?"

"I have *many* specialties, but yes, opening crash-bar doors with a coat hanger is one of them. However, Mr. Suddenly-Likes-to-Plan-Things, look how far that entrance is from the photographs."

"It's not that much farther and you only have two turns."

"Running *toward* the security guards."

"Your way, they're coming up behind you. Like you're running away from them. This way, you see them coming, you can get away easier." Sawyer looked down the hall, estimating distances. "You could sprint from the school entrance to the hall in like ten seconds. It'll take five seconds each to cut the wires. Then you hit the exit. You're in and out in thirty seconds."

"You have to add in the time it takes to get the doors open. And that's two sets."

"So you're thinking about ninety seconds?"

"No way," she said. "It has to be less than that. Fifty seconds. Tops."

"You could do it. But only if you go my way."

Grace looked at the map, tracing his route with her little finger. "You know something, you're right. And if I get to this point here before they get to the main entrance, they might not even see me go down the hallway where the photographs are."

"And if the guard office is where I think it is, they'd have to cover twice the distance you have to cover. That may make it easier for you to outrun them if you have to." He reached down and brushed his fingers against the polished tile. "This type of floor can be really slippery."

"No problem. I've got a pair of black Adidas trainers from dance class."

He gave her a sideways glance.

"Yeah, dance class. I'm full of surprises."

He shook his head and tapped a finger on the map. "I'm just thinking that if it was suddenly slipperier where the guards had to run, it'd give you a lot more time."

She smiled, the ends of her mouth curling up. "Careful, there's a word for people like you."

"Planners?"

"Accessories."

CHAPTER

30

THE SCHOOL WAS empty.

There were eight people in his economics class, thirteen in history, seven in Spanish, and an impressive twenty-one in English, but that included three juniors who got a pass from study hall to come in and watch the second half of *Shakespeare in Love*.

The last day before a five-day break.

Most of the missing were off on family getaways, beaching out and tanning up or hitting the slopes to nail a boneless McTwist or some other snowboard trick they would go on about for months. The rest of the students had either convinced their parents that nothing important would happen in school that day, which was the truth, or that the administration decided to close school a day early, which was true enough.

By unspoken agreement, those left behind conspired to do as little as possible. Students went to class, teachers took attendance, and neither group did anything to upset the balance. On Monday the truce would be over and it would be back to normal, but nobody was thinking that far ahead.

It was an A day on the rotating schedule. It had been an A day on Monday, too, and it would be an A day again when they started back up after Thanksgiving, more evidence that they were simply marking time until the others returned.

Sawyer swung by his locker to drop off the *Norton Anthology of American Literature* he didn't need for English and pick up the calculator and notebook he wouldn't need for math. Walking around school with nothing in his hands would have only reminded him that there was no reason to be there. There wasn't, but carrying something made it easier to deal with. He was making the switch when Renée walked up.

"Surprised to see you here," she said.

"Where else am I going to be?"

"I don't know, maybe at home, pining away for Zoë."

"Pining away?"

"It was in the movie we watched in trig."

"Have you heard from her?"

"Please. She texts every five minutes—having a margarita, lounging by the pool, talking to some hot college guys, going clubbing, doing shots," she said, changing her voice to let him know she found the messages oh-so whatever.

Zoë had texted him, too; quick little "miss-you"s with frowny faces, updates about the heat and wind and a few about how her parents wouldn't let her out of their sight, blaming it all on somebody named Van der Sloot. And he had texted back with required "miss-you"s of his own, avoiding any lies. Well, big ones, anyway.

"She's going to be there the whole week. Do you know how tan she's going to be?"

"Go to a tanning booth."

"It's not the same," Renée said, and then without pausing, "I saw you on the road yesterday."

She didn't have to say the rest. She had seen him driving around with a girl in the car that wasn't Zoë. Why else would she have brought it up? There was nothing mean in the way she said it, she wasn't accusing him of anything, not threatening to tell Zoë or plotting with him to keep it a secret, she was just putting it out there, making a simple observation, like telling him that the sky was blue, no judging at all.

Right.

"It was that Grace girl, the Westie, wasn't it?"

He bumped his locker door with a bang and Renée smiled.

"I work with her grandfather. He asked me to give her a ride after school."

"Don't worry, I won't tell Zoë," she said, and Sawyer knew then that she already had.

Mr. Young was standing in the front of the class, remote in hand, ready to start *Good Will Hunting*, when Sawyer walked into the room. He knew he wasn't late, but the way Mr. Young was looking at him it was obvious something was up.

"Sawyer?" Mr. Young picked a paper off his desk, skimmed it, and looked back. "What are you doing here?"

"It's an A day, isn't it?"

"Yes, it is, but didn't the guidance office tell you?" He brought the paper over and handed it to Sawyer. "You're not in this class anymore."

Sawyer knew the rest. But he listened anyway, eyes on the paper, not reading.

"Ms. Coville sent me that email this morning. I would've thought you'd know all about it."

"Yeah. I do. I guess I just forgot."

Mr. Young sighed and shrugged, both more than the moment required. "She explained how you want to focus on your *other* classes. But you know, Sawyer, you were really turning things around in *this* class. Look at that last test. You aced it." He took the paper back, folding it in half and stuffing it in his shirt pocket. "But I guess you gotta do what you gotta do."

Sawyer said nothing, and when Mr. Young told him he was supposed to go to the guidance office so they could put him in a study hall, he nodded, headed down the hall, and out the side door to the parking lot.

CHAPTER
31

"GO AHEAD," GRACE said, "slide it in."

Sawyer hesitated. "It's going to be tight."

"Just shove it in, it'll fit. Trust me, I've done this plenty of times."

He took a deep breath, shifted his position, and pushed.

"That's it," she said. "A little to the left. Down. That's it."

Sawyer tightened his grip, then pulled on the wire coat hanger. The crash bar clicked down and the narrow space between the doors widened as Grace pulled on the outside handle.

"Ta-da," she said, applauding. "With a little practice you could turn pro."

Sawyer stood up, the hook end of the straightened

hanger slipping off the crash bar. "   the
at West?"

"Had to teach myself. Lost my key
times. But it comes in handy."

"I can bet."

"The one at the library was even easier than th.
let the door swing closed, locking them outside. She
her finger down the gap between the two glass doors. ".
was twice as wide as this. I could get my pinky in there.
They really need to renovate that place."

"Leave a note when you bring the painting back."

"Please. They haven't even noticed it yet. I mean,
come on, folks, help a girl out here."

Sawyer wiggled the hook of the coat hanger back
between the doors. "The museum is going to have newer
doors. What if there's no gap?"

"There's *always* a gap, you just have to make it bigger."

"Dynamite?"

"Sneaker." She grabbed hold of the left handle, then
swung a leg up, bracing her foot against the handle on
the right side door. She leaned back and pushed out
with her leg. The gap widened. She took the hanger
from him and worked it into position, popping the
door open. It took less than five seconds. "At one with

force am I, young Skywalker."

"It's kinda risky," he said. "You might not weigh nough to get the museum doors apart."

"I'll take that as a compliment. And you're not an actuary yet so no lectures on risk."

"Change of plans," he said, enjoying the thought. "I'm not cut out for the wild life of an insurance actuary."

"Party *animals*. That's the word on the street. Stick with something simple."

"Like art theft?"

"I was going to say underwater welding. Besides, the way you work that coat hanger, you'd starve."

"Yeah, you wish."

"No, I wish you were faster, that's what I wish. If you were any slower you'd be *part* of the door."

"Thirty seconds. That's all it'll take."

"I'm sorry, did you say thirty *minutes*? That's more your speed."

"Thirty seconds," Sawyer said, snatching the hanger, smiling his best shark grin.

Grace took out her phone and thumbed the stopwatch app. "Okay, Houdini, thirty seconds."

"Hold on. What's the bet?"

She held up her phone, showing all zeros on the counter. "Loser picks the next movie."

"That's not fair. You *like* picking out movies."

"True," she said. "But I don't like losing."

CHAPTER
32

TUESDAY NIGHT WAS a blur, a marathon of online games and text messages that ended when he heard his parents getting ready for work Wednesday morning.

He headed to the gym for the first time in months. The place was filled with retirees doing ten-pound curls and stay-at-home moms sweating up the leg machines. It wasn't a good workout, but it helped him burn off some of the frustration he hadn't noticed he felt.

Back at home, shaved, showered, and dressed, Sawyer poured a bowl of cereal and scrolled through the texts from the night before.

The first dozen had come one right after the other, all of them focused on the facts—*who was she, where were you going, what did she say, what did you do, how long were you there.* Spread out over the next hour were accusations disguised as questions—*what did I tell you about her, how come you keep running into her, why would you talk to her, doesn't she know you have a girlfriend.* After midnight, they started to change. The spelling and grammar got sloppy, even for Zoë, and he could read the slur in her voice that told him she was at a club—*how cld u do this too me, I dont need u, shes a BITCH, ur an asshole.* He'd gotten a text at one thirty—*DONOT TALK TO THAT BITCH AGAIN!!!*—and another around two— *I HATE U*—then the phone went quiet. It had been close to five in morning, when he was about to crack the prestige level on *Black Ops*, when the texts started back up—*I get mad cuz ur not with me, guys here are such LOSERS, I want to walk on the beach with you, I don't like rum, wish you were here, miss you, don't talk to her again.*

Zoë hadn't broken up with him, but he knew now that it was only a matter of time before it was over.

And when that time came, he knew that he'd be the one to end it.

There were no new texts. If she was sleeping it off, then he wouldn't hear from her again till late afternoon at the earliest. That gave him hours.

He went online, found what he was looking for, and

downloaded it, then sent a text of his own. Less than a minute later he had a response.

It made him smile.

"What did you think?"

"Are you *kidding*? It was great. I can't believe I never saw it before."

He shook his head and laughed. "What do they teach you over at West?"

It had taken him only fifty-six seconds to get the wire hanger in the gap, the hook around the crash bar, and the door at her aunt's apartment building open. And that, Grace was quick to point out, was twenty-six seconds too long. So he lost the bet and had to get the movie—and before he hit the Play button on his laptop, before he had even picked her up at the Dunkin' Donuts, he knew she'd love it.

Butch Cassidy and the Sundance Kid.

It was a Western and it was in color, two things she didn't expect, but it starred the main actors from *The Sting* and it had the same smartass/cool guy/way-too-smooth sense of humor. A couple of buddies on the wrong side of the law, with gunfights, explosions, and a big finish. He'd heard about it years ago, his father saying it was his favorite movie of all time, but other than short clips between long commercial breaks on AMC, Sawyer had never seen it. His father was right, it was a good movie. Not the best ever but on the list, sure. And Sawyer was glad he had seen it with Grace.

"I like how they got away at the end," she said, sipping her warm diet cream soda.

Sawyer turned to look at her. "*Got away?* Did I miss something?"

"When they came running out shooting," she said, her free hand flying, an imaginary pistol picking off targets around the room.

"They were surrounded."

She nodded, still shooting. "Yeah, but they could get away. There weren't *that* many people shooting at them."

"It was the entire Bolivian Army."

"Maybe," Grace said, squinting, taking one last shot. "But they didn't show them getting killed, did they?"

"It was a freeze-frame that faded to black," Sawyer said, using the terms he had learned from her. "I think it's pretty obvious what happened next."

"It's open to interpretation. And I interpret it to mean that they got away."

"I don't think that's what the director had in mind."

She took another sip of her soda, set the can down on the floor, then punched him in the arm. "*That's* why you wanted me to see it. So I could see what happens to the wicked who are lured into a life of crime."

"No," he said, forcing himself not to rub his arm. "It's just a movie I like."

"Which coincidently happens to be about two robbers who get killed."

"By the Bolivian Army. If you were planning something in Lima I could see the connection."

"It's a metaphor."

"It's a movie."

"You're trying to scare me straight."

"I like you twisted."

"Lima's in Peru."

He slumped back against the couch, wondering why he couldn't stop smiling. She leaned forward to read the time in the corner of the laptop screen. "It's three twenty. What time will your parents get home?"

"Not till after five. And so what if they do?"

"Alone in the house with a girl that's not your girlfriend? A girl they never met? A Westie? How you think *that's* going to look?"

"What do I care? If I want to have a friend over to watch a movie, that's my business."

"Ya think?"

He thought, then sighed. "No, probably not."

"Ah, yes. The old 'as long as you live under my roof' story. I know it well. But that's all right, you've got it good here."

He gave her a look, one eyebrow rising on its own.

"Oh, please," she said. "Beautiful house, sweet car, decent parents—"

"Who want to run my life."

"That's *every* parent." She waved it off as meaningless. "So they're a little overprotective. They'll grow out of it. Maybe. Besides, you'll be in college next year. They gotta let go by then. I think it's a law."

He clicked his laptop shut. "I told them that I'm not going to Wembly."

"How'd it go over?"

He shrugged.

She smiled at that. "You're taking quite a risk, bucko."

"I've stolen an international treaty, I've used spy glasses to cheat on a test, and I've driven the getaway car for an art thief," he said, counting them off on his fingers. "I guess I'm ready for it."

"What's your hottie girlfriend think about this new plan of yours?"

Sawyer shook his head, laughing to himself, wondering if everybody thought he was that whipped, and knowing they probably did. "She'll be pissed, but she'll get over it. Or not. Whatever."

"Uh-oh, sounds like trouble in paradise. You worried she's banging some cabana boy at the beach club?"

"It's not what you're thinking."

"Trust me," Grace said, and smiled over the top of her cream soda can. "You've got no idea what I'm thinking."

CHAPTER
33

SOMEHOW 4:20 A.M. came earlier than normal.

When the alarm went off it was impossibly dark, and he was certain he had screwed it up, setting it for one thirty by mistake. But he had been awake at one thirty— eyes closed, mind racing—stuff too stupid to think about during the day keeping him up all night, stuff about calculus tests and libraries and old movies and Zoë and Grace and plans, *lots* of plans, ridiculous plans, plans that were brilliant at two fifty and forgotten by three, replaced by other plans that were total genius for the ten minutes they lasted.

Two rough nights in a row. Not a record, but he knew the lack of sleep would start to catch up to him.

Sawyer blamed his father. He knew it wasn't his

father's fault, but he was in the mood to blame him for everything and, just like the plans that raced through his head, it made sense at the time.

All his father had done was to remind him about something he didn't need to be reminded about—"Don't forget to set your alarm, son. It's going to be a busy day at St. Mary's, and they're going to need your help."

Sawyer almost said "If it's going to be so busy, why don't you come with me?" but he realized just in time that it would be exactly the kind of thing his father *would* do. As tough as it was going to be spending the morning prepping for the big Thanksgiving Day meal at the soup kitchen, Sawyer knew it would be worse having his father next to him, telling him what to do, even though he'd been doing it just fine for months. So instead Sawyer said that the alarm was already set and that he'd have no problem getting there on time. Which was easy to say at nine p.m.

The streets were empty, but the small parking lot next to the church was almost full. The team at the kitchen had said that this would happen, that dozens of people would show up that morning, all wanting to help so that they could tell their friends about doing one day of community service with the unfortunates at a soup kitchen on the west edge of the city. St. Mary's wouldn't turn them away, just like they wouldn't turn away anyone coming to eat, but these twice-a-year volunteers—Thanksgiving and Christmas—would make it all more complicated than it had to be.

It was a good half hour before the kitchen started serving, but there were already a handful of bundled-up shapes shuffling around in the alcove by the front door. Sawyer saw some he recognized—Larry Long Coat, Cowboy Kurt, Angelo, Hey-Howdie Man, Lucy, Tom the Dolphins Fan, Mrs. Morton—and a lot more he didn't. He waved and a few waved back as he walked to the entrance at the side of the building.

"Hey, Sawyer. Thanks for coming in." Tonisha put a checkmark next to his name on her clipboard. First year out of college, five years older than him, tops, and she ran the whole program. "We've got a lot of volunteers today. I want to make them feel welcome so I'm putting most of them out front. You okay with that?"

He was okay with that. Out front meant working the line, serving food, clearing tables, refilling the milk machine, making coffee. Out front meant getting to talk with the people who came in, hearing the stories, the jokes, the thanks. Sawyer understood why Tonisha would want the regulars in the back and the one-shot volunteers out front. Being out front, you felt like you were doing something worth doing, making a difference in somebody's life. A small difference, but a good one.

It was the kind of feeling that might get you to volunteer more than twice a year.

It's what kept him coming back.

That, and his father.

Tonisha had him down for scrape-and-load. Not the kind of job that brought in the volunteers. The dirty dishes would come in from the cafeteria through the low window, he'd hose them off, set them on the rack, and run them though the dishwasher. It was loud and hot, and even with the white St. Mary's apron on and the splash guards up around the sink, you couldn't help getting wet.

The cook was a big guy named Wayne, a lot of fun but serious when it came to the food. He had the new people chopping celery for the salads that would go with the Thanksgiving meal. When he saw Sawyer he gave a slow nod and brought his chopping knife down hard on a carrot, then held up his hand, middle finger bent back out of view, every one of the volunteers at the table gasping. It was his favorite trick and he sold it, eyes all wide and his other hand still holding the knife. The first ten times he saw it, Sawyer fell for it too. Wayne held his pose a bit longer, then flipped up his missing finger, getting them all laughing, breaking the ice. He was good at that teamwork stuff.

"Happy Thanksgiving, Sawyer," Nellie said, pushing a cart loaded with dirty pots across the floor. "Now how about you getting to work?"

It stayed busy after that, first all the pans and bowls and giant mixing spoons from the kitchen, then the plates and glasses and silverware from the cafeteria. People would come up to the long opening and he'd see their hands as they set their trays down on the metal table, pushing them through to the sink, somebody bending over now and then to shout in a thanks or to compliment the chef, and he'd yell something back even though he doubted they could hear him over the noise. Ten minutes and the bottom of his jeans were soaked through, twenty minutes and water squished out of his Chuck Taylors with every step.

He slipped three times on the soapy floor before the idea clicked and he mentally added another item to Grace's shopping list.

Regular mornings he'd be done by eight and off to school, but today was different, and when Tonisha came by with his replacement, it was already past noon. She put her arm around Sawyer's shoulder, pulling him in for a buddy hug. "Thanks for sticking around," she said, pushing a wayward dread back up under her hairnet. "Sad to say, but it's our busiest day of the year. You going to get something to eat?"

"No, I can't eat here."

"Don't tell that to Wayne. At least not when he's holding a knife. He takes that kind of comment personally."

"What I meant was my family's going to my aunt's house for dinner."

She smiled. "That's good. You should be with your family today."

"Yeah, I guess."

"What do you mean, you *guess*? Of course you should," she said, sliding her arm off his shoulder and grabbing his hand, steering him around the steamy, spitting dishwasher to the low window by the sink, pulling him down so they could see out between the growing stacks of dirty dishes. It was the first chance he had to look all morning.

The place was packed.

Every table taken and a dozen people in line, trays in hand.

Whites, blacks, Hispanics, Asians.

Everybody.

Jeans and sweatpants, yeah, but some women in dresses, a few men wearing ties, an old guy in a baggy suit. And lots of families.

Looking just like any family.

Like his family.

And kids everywhere. Running around between the rows, sitting at the tables, all smiles and laughing, playing with other kids' toys, having a great time.

It was different for their parents.

This wasn't the regular crowd. There were no shopping carts, no battered backpacks, nobody looking like they'd need to be getting a free meal at a church.

But then, there they were.

"You see all those folks? Do you think any of them want to be spending their Thanksgiving with a bunch of

243

strangers? *Please.* At least they've got their families with them. Mostly. The ones who come in alone? That's gotta be rough."

They were easy to spot.

Sitting as far away from anybody as they could, setting themselves apart from the families and from each other, eyes on their plates or staring out at nothing, wolfing their food down and bolting out or eating so slowly it was as if they never wanted to finish. It was mostly men, older, his father's age, but there were some women, just as old, some younger men in their twenties, and a few guys in their teens.

And one lone girl.

Purple jacket.

Red scarf.

Black beret.

Head down.

So small she was easy to miss, easy to ignore.

"It's like that poster over by Father Mull's office," Tonisha said. "How's it go? 'To the world they're a nobody, but to somebody they're the world.'"

That girl? Grace? She's a nobody.

Tonisha gave his hand a squeeze and said something about how thankful she was for her regulars and something else about prayers that he didn't hear, and the next minute she was over by the ovens, joking with Wayne. Sawyer's mind was still out in the dining area.

He knew what he had to do.

It wasn't going to be easy, hell no, and he didn't want to do it, he wanted to do the exact opposite, but it was one of his friends out there, all alone.

No, that wasn't right.

It wasn't one of his friends.

It was his best friend.

And you did things for a best friend that you didn't want to do because you knew that's what your best friend would want you to do, would need you to do.

Sawyer knew what he had to do.

It was the same thing he'd want Grace to do if it was him out there at the table and her back here, watching him.

He took off his apron and hung it with the others, slung his coat over his shoulder, took a deep, long, shaky breath.

You can do this, he told himself.

And then he did.

He pushed open the door and sprinted out to his car, driving off before Grace knew he was there.

CHAPTER 34

SHE POINTED A knife at Sawyer.

"One, you got ripped off. And two, this turkey is delicious."

His aunt was right, he did get ripped off, but things had changed since he made that bet and he had other plans now, plans that had nothing to do with precalc or Wembly, plans they didn't know about. Sure, there was a lot to do—applications to fill out, forms to send in, online admissions essays to write—but he'd get it done. That was the plan. Well, one of them.

"He didn't get ripped off," his father said. "He lost a bet. We agreed he had to get an A and he didn't. But you're right about the turkey."

It was Sawyer, his parents, Grandma Edith, Aunt Paula, Uncle Rick, and their three girls—Megan and Shannon, who were still kids, and Erin, who was only thirteen but looked as old as Grace and acted older than Zoë—all sitting around the formal dining-room table his aunt used as her home office. The stacks of papers and files that normally covered the table were missing, the computer and printer moved to the floor by the china cabinet, but it still felt like her office. It was sticky warm in the room, with the gas fireplace going and the steam from the kitchen and everybody just a little too close.

Physically, anyway.

And it was noisy, too, the TV on, the Lions losing to an empty room, tinny Christmas music coming from the cheap computer speakers, Misty barking in the garage, everybody talking—everybody but his cousin Erin and him. She was busy texting a boy her parents didn't like and he was busy thinking about a girl his parents didn't know existed.

"Sawyer, didn't you say you got an A-plus?"

"It was an eighty-six," his father said. "The teacher marked it on a curve. It wasn't a *real* A."

"Oh. An *eighty*-six." His aunt took a sip of her wine.

"Well, that's still a good grade."

"It's very good. It's outstanding. But it's not an A."

He was sure Grace hadn't seen him when he snuck out. She still had a full plate in front of her and there were too many people by the main door for her to see him run by. Driving home, all he wanted to do was go back, sit down next to her, maybe put his arm around her shoulder, tell her . . . what? That there was nothing to be embarrassed about, that a lot of people had to go to soup kitchens now, that she could spend Thanksgiving with him, that he didn't care where she came from or what school she went to or what her family was like or that people thought she was a nobody?

Yeah, that would have gone over well.

"But I'll say this for him, he took the loss like a man. Didn't whine about it, didn't get all pissed off. He accepted it and moved on. Right, son?"

Sawyer smiled. Why not? If that's the way his father wanted to remember it, that was fine by him. Besides, he owed his father one. If his father *had* lived up to the bet, there was no guarantee that he wouldn't change his mind later. It had happened before. This way Sawyer knew where he stood. It had only taken a couple hours online to see that he didn't need his parents to get him into a school, that there were options, lots of them, and okay, some of them weren't as good as Wembly—not even close—but they were his options.

"So if Sawyer lost," Uncle Rick said, "what did you win?"

"*I* didn't win anything. It was Sawyer who really won. He got to drop precalculus."

Uncle Rick laughed at that. "You got an A and you *dropped* the class?"

"It really *wasn't* an A," his aunt said. "More like a B-plus. Which is still good. But it's not an A."

"I never got above a D in calculus and I couldn't get out of it. Almost kept me from getting into college."

Sawyer knew that his parents would be giving him that now-do-you-understand? look, so he kept focused on the turkey, which really was delicious. He wondered what Grace had thought of Wayne's cooking.

"Speaking of which, your mother told me the good news."

He looked up at his aunt, then around at the others, trying to think of what the good news could be.

"College? That letter?"

"Oh, yeah," Sawyer said. "I got accepted at Wembly."

"Well, you could at least *try* to sound excited."

"I'm sure he is. Do you know what you're going to major in yet?"

"Probably accounting," his mother said. "He's thinking of becoming an insurance actuary. He even wrote a paper on it."

"I don't even know what that is," his aunt said.

"Yes, you do. They work for insurance companies and they—"

"Let *him* tell it, Rick. Go on, Sawyer."

Sawyer laughed to himself. He had written the career paper that morning. It took him all of fifteen minutes to find it, download it, change a few words, and turn it in to his parents for their approval. He planted enough mistakes to give his mother something to find, and after ten minutes of pulling those out and pasting the original stuff back in, it was done. One day he'd tell them the truth about the paper, maybe even about the precalc test. But that was years away, after he'd graduated from a college he hadn't found yet and earned a degree in a field he probably hadn't even considered.

"Insurance actuaries evaluate risks," Sawyer said, picturing the Wikipedia entry. "They determine strategies that will maximize gain and minimize losses using analytical skills that help them predict outcomes. And they're experts at understanding human behavior, too. They know what you're going to do before you even know you want to do it."

"Wow, did you hear that, Erin?" His aunt turned to look at her daughter, who did her best to ignore that end of the room. "Sawyer, that's *really* interesting. I'd never heard of that before."

"So, basically," his uncle said, waving his fork, "actuaries spend half their day imagining shitty situations, then the other half making plans to avoid them. Sound like you, Sawyer?"

"Yeah," Sawyer said. "It's starting to."

His father poured the last of the wine into his glass. "Don't let him kid you, Rick. Sawyer's not afraid of hard work. He's been up since, what, four? Volunteering over at St. Mary's. The soup kitchen."

Aunt Paula smiled at him. "That's *fantastic*. Really, it is. I mean, what kid does any volunteering anymore?"

His cousin Erin, unimpressed, glared down the table. "We *all* have to volunteer. It's a school requirement."

"Yes, I *know*," Aunt Paula said, matching the attitude. "But *some* students are willing to volunteer even when it doesn't fit nicely into their social schedule."

His uncle jumped in between them. "Lot of people there today?"

Sawyer nodded. "Lot more than usual."

"That's good. I mean that you were there for them. It's a shame anybody has to go there, but you know what I mean."

"I'm very proud of him," his mom said, reaching around his father to pat him on the back.

"That meal? That could have been the best thing to happen to some of them all month," Uncle Rick said. "The thing is, you never know who you're helping, or how much it means to them. You could've changed somebody's life."

Erin rolled her eyes. "Yeah, a dead turkey saves the world."

"Seriously, Sawyer, what you're doing, going in at four in the morning, it's really important. You're making a difference. Even if it's just one person."

He mumbled something that could pass as a "thanks," thinking about one person and the difference she made.

"Speaking of four in the morning," Aunt Paula said to his mother, "please tell me you're not going to be one of the crazies waiting for some store to open."

"No, I did my last Black Friday years ago. I wonder how many people are going to get crushed this year."

"The traffic jams, the accidents—"

"The fights over some toy."

"Plus all that crowd control."

"I'd hate to be a policeman tonight," Aunt Paula said, then said something about the weather being good for shopping, and that got his father going on about a guy at work who loved Black Friday but hated Christmas, and that started Megan and Shannon in on what they wanted Santa to bring them, while Uncle Rick inched up the volume on the game and the dog started barking again.

Sawyer had stopped listening, busy revising a plan.

HE TYPED Happy Thanksgiving, then hit Send.

Back at you, pilgrim. How was your aunt's?

OK.

That's it?

The turkey was good.

So was the one we had.

He smiled. He'd have to let Wayne know.

Lot of family at your aunt's?

Just the rents, aunt/uncle, Gram, and my cousins, he typed, then added a question he knew the answer to, but if he didn't ask, it'd seem weird. How about you?

Packed.

Fun?

Of course. If it wasn't fun . . .

You wouldn't go. For a second he imagined that she did have fun, that she was just early, that her family all arrived after he bolted, that she knew other people who were there, good people who were making it through some tough times, that she got to laugh and joke around and be the center of attention, famous in her own way, rich in the things people say really matter. But it wasn't like that and he knew it, and that kept him texting. Doing anything tonight?

Can't go to my aunt's. She has "company."

We can go shopping.

It's Thanksgiving. Nothing's open.

Later. Like 3am.

R U insane? It's Black Friday.

I know. Could be fun.

She texted **Ever done it?** Then, before he could send his smartass response, she wrote **I mean shopping on Black Friday.**

No.

I did once. It's crazy. There was like a riot at the Target over here. I almost got my leg broken because some bubba wanted to save fifty bucks on a big screen.

There were cops there, right?

Tons of them.

Only at that Target?

No, everywhere. Don't you watch the news? It's like the biggest shopping time all year.

And a lot of cars on the street?

Traffic jams by the malls. Nothing moves in or out of them.

So I guess the cops are really busy.

Yeah. It's like that all night on Black Friday, she texted, and he waited. It took her longer than he thought it would, but she caught up.

OMG! U R brilliant!

What time do I pick you up?

Another pause, this one stretching out over two minutes, then, **I'm all set.**

He read the text twice.

It was ridiculous.

How could she be all set? She lived ten miles from the art museum. He texted back. I don't mind. Spent the whole day with family. I need to get out of the house.

Go see a movie.

I'd rather go "shopping."

Go ahead. But I'm all set. Thanks, though.

Don't you need a ride?

She ignored the question and typed, **I'll call you in the morning with the juicy details.**

"All set"?

What was she going to do, take a bus? Hitchhike? The first was ridiculous, the second was stupid. And he could see her doing them both. Then he thought of a third.

Maybe she had convinced someone else to give her a ride.

Some guy from a date gone wrong.

A guy who'd give her a ride, no questions asked.

A guy who'd expect something in return.

Who thought no meant maybe.

Let me drive you there.

No response.

You need me.

Nothing.

Five minutes later, he sent the last text.

It's my plan too.

He watched his screen for thirty minutes. She didn't write back.

CHAPTER
36

SAWYER FOUND A parking space on a residential street, five blocks from the art museum. He would have liked it better if there hadn't been streetlights, but there were enough cars so that no one would notice his, and with the bars closing there were even a few people on the streets, groups talking louder than they realized, or strays, like him, walking fast and alone.

He wasn't tired but he should have been. He hadn't slept much the last couple nights, and he was at St. Mary's at five that morning, but after telling his mother he was going to be one of the first in line at Best Buy—great deal on a tablet!—he had climbed into bed and stared at the ceiling, piecing things together until the alarm went off at two. He got dressed again—dark jeans, black

T-shirt, black sweatshirt, dark blue coat—stuffed a knit cap in one pocket and pair of gloves in the other, and headed out. Ten minutes later he stopped at an all-night 7-Eleven, then headed west into the city.

Aunt Paula had been right, there were a lot of cars on the road. Most were pulling off at the exit near the mall, but there was enough other traffic so his car didn't stand out. By two thirty he was parked and making his way down the sidewalk toward the back of the art museum. His aunt was right about the weather, too. It was cold but not freezing, the heavy cloud cover keeping the temperature up, which was good, and blocking out the moon and stars, which was even better.

He knew where she'd be—in the shadows near the air-conditioning unit, up close to the shrubs—and he knew she'd wait till three before she made her move.

That was the plan.

At least, the plan she told him.

Sawyer cut through the synagogue parking lot, crossed an empty street, hopped the waist-high fence without breaking stride, and blended into the blackness that bordered the back of the building. He leaned against the side of a tree, waiting for his eyes to adjust, and when three minutes passed and he couldn't see any better, he started toward the darker shapes that he hoped were bushes. It was farther away than he thought, the dried-up, hard lawn going on and on and on, him out there, in the shadows, yeah, but nothing to hide behind or duck into, exposed if someone knew where to look. And it would be just as big and open and exposed when she came running out, something he didn't think she'd planned on.

It felt like it took an hour, but it was closer to thirty seconds.

He got to the row of head-high bushes and slid between the first two, slow and silent, the branches barely moving, stepping onto the narrow path that ran the length of the room-sized air-conditioning unit. He leaned against the tall metal side and waited, listening for footsteps, hearing only his muffled breathing, his eyes straining to separate the shades of black on black.

Then something moved.

His fists balled up and he eased off his heels, ready if he was wrong, and willed his voice to a whisper.

"Hey," he said, then jerked his head back as something sharp and cold pushed up under his chin, holding there, tilting him off balance. He swallowed hard, the sound loud in the silence, and tried again.

"Grace. It's me. Sawyer."

He could feel the point against his skin, the end of a straightened wire coat hanger digging in. Then the shadow moved and the point was gone.

"What the hell are you doing here?" Her voice was low, her words whispered with a hard edge, a quiet yell.

"I wanted to make sure you were okay."

She breathed louder than she spoke. "I'm fine. Now go away."

"How'd you get here?"

"I took the bus, what do you think? Now just go."

"All right. But I'll wait here till you come out, just in case they're chasing you."

"*What?* No. Get outta here."

"I can distract them."

"Don't you get it? I'm about to commit a crime."

"I know what I'm doing," he said.

"You're *this close* to being an accessory."

She couldn't see the smile on his face, the way he shook his head at the thought. "I've been an accessory for years. I'm upgrading to accomplice."

"No, you're not. This is a one-person plan," she

whispered as she poked a finger at his chest. "*I* get in, *I* run down the hall, *I* cut the wires, *I* get the picture, *I* get out the door, and *I* get away. This is *my* plan."

Sawyer sighed. "Yeah. I know."

"Now leave. I'll call you later." She turned to go, and then he remembered.

"Hold on. I got this for you." He reached inside his jacket, pulled out a plastic bottle, and handed it to her. He'd bought the smallest one, but it looked huge in her hands.

"What is it?"

"Dish soap. When you go down that last hall, pour it on the floor behind you. They run on that, they'll go flying."

There was a pause, then, almost laughing, she said, "Clever. Really, it is. But it won't work."

"Trust me, it will."

Grace shook the bottle. It was full so it didn't make a sound. "So now you're an expert on soap?"

"No, on slipping."

"What do you know," she said, that laugh in her voice. "You really *are* an insurance actuary."

"No, I'm just a dishwasher at Saint Mary's soup

kitchen," he said, the words tumbling out before he could stop them. Later, he would think of all the things he should have said, but at that dark, dead-quiet moment, he couldn't think of anything.

Another pause—a longer, awful pause—hung in the air between them, then three tiny electric beeps broke the silence. Grace pulled back her sleeve and checked the illuminated dial of her watch.

"Showtime."

She pulled off her knit cap, stuffed it in her backpack, and put on her black beret.

"You can't wear that," he said. "Your face will show on the cameras."

"I won't be looking at the cameras. Besides, it's my lucky hat."

He nodded. "Don't forget to have fun."

"I always do," she said, and even in the darkness he could see her smile. She turned and stepped toward an opening in the bushes, then stopped and reached back. "Here," Grace said, handing him the plastic bottle. "It's not part of the plan." He felt her gloved hand slide off the bottle and squeeze his arm. "But thanks for thinking of me."

Sawyer watched as, crouching low, she went straight

for the set of glass doors of the museum's back entrance, the same ones he'd come through when the school bus dropped off his class in fifth grade. The bright lights around the entrance made the night seem darker. And then there she was, out of the shadows and up to the doors, kneeling down, wiggling the hook end of the straightened coat hanger between the crash-bar doors.

Only it wasn't working.

The coat hanger wasn't wiggling through.

He watched as Grace tried bracing against the L-shaped door handle, leveraging more space, but she didn't have the weight to move it.

"Come on, push," Sawyer whispered, watching, his muscles tensing as he mirrored her motions, his mind racing with things she had taught him about doors and gaps.

She switched sides, putting a foot up against the door handle, then switched back, going at it again, the hanger clattering against the glass.

It was taking too long.

Her plan falling apart before it got started.

She had to be inside by now if this was going to work.

It was as good as over.

He started running.

Grace pressed her shoulder against the glass, her dance-class trainers slipping on dirty concrete, and she gasped when he reached around her and grabbed the handle. Eyes wide, she looked up at him.

"Sawyer, no."

He braced his foot against the other handle, the paper-thin gap widening as he pushed and pulled. He looked at her and smiled. "Now, you ready for this?"

She hesitated, then wiggled the straightened coat hanger between the doors, snagging the crash bar with the hook, pulling it toward her, the first door popping open.

Fifty seconds.

Grace darted in, then Sawyer, grabbing the handle on the second set of doors. Grace worked the hanger through, and when it popped open and Sawyer ran in first, Grace didn't stop him. They were inside now, running together down the long, dimly lit corridor, racing past dark paintings and white statues and the blinking red lights on the security cameras.

Thirty seconds.

They had made the first turn and could see the hallway with the photographs when the alarm went off.

"Keep going," Sawyer shouted over the high-pitched

buzz, slowing down to snap the top off the plastic bottle, rolling it back across the smooth tile floor that led to the main gallery.

Twenty seconds.

He caught up to Grace as she ducked into the dark passage. "This one," she said, stopping halfway down the hall, handing him the wire cutters as she held up the frame.

In the distance, under the alarm, they could hear shouting.

Ten seconds.

Both hands on the grips, he snapped through one wire, then heard a crash and someone swearing and knew the soap had worked.

Six seconds.

He snapped the second wire and Grace swept the photograph away.

Four.

"Let's go," she said, running for the exit at the end of the hall.

Three.

Behind them someone yelled stop.

Two.

They hit the crash bar together, bursting out into the

cold darkness, a new alarm going off as they jumped over the short ramp, Grace grabbing his hand and pulling him close, looking into his eyes, holding them, smiling, her eyes lighting up like the first time they met, then Grace shouting "I'm sorry, Sawyer," as the spotlights from a half-dozen police cars lit up the night.

CHAPTER 37

"I JUST WANT to know one thing," the assistant district attorney said, flipping through the papers in the manila folder on his desk. "What were you thinking?"

It was a good question. It was the same thing his parents wanted to know, the same question Zoë had asked the one time she had answered her phone. And it was the same question he'd been asking himself since he was facedown on the cold, hard ground, hands out to his sides where they could see them.

He had had a lot of time to think of an answer.

The hour he had sat alone in the back of the police cruiser at the art museum.

The three hours on that bench, next to the Black Friday shoplifters.

Standing against the gray wall for the mug shots.

Wiping the black fingerprint ink off his hands.

Waiting for the judge to read the charges.

Waiting in line to call his parents.

The hours and hours and hours sitting in his room at home, sitting at the attorney's office, sitting at the kitchen table as his parents talked and yelled and cried.

He had had a lot of time—and they had a lot of questions—but no one in the room expected him to have any answers. Not the ADA, not his attorney, not his parents.

Thing was, he had a good answer for every question they asked.

Why did he open the doors, why did he pour soap on the floor, why did he cut down the photograph, why did he put his whole future at risk.

And he had good answers for the questions they *didn't* ask, too.

Why did he help her steal the Model UN treaty, why did he cheat on the precalc test, why did he agree to drive her to the library that night when he knew she was going to steal a painting, why did he help cover up the crime by kissing her when the police car drove by, why would he want to hang around with that girl in the first place.

So yeah, he had answers, but they would only make everything worse.

"I assume, Ms. Dixon, that you've gone over all this with your client?"

"We have. And thanks again for allowing the parents to sit in today."

"No problem. As long as they understand that he's an adult and he'll be charged as such." Then he looked past Sawyer and said, "I'm sure that this is a difficult time for you."

Sawyer was tempted to turn around and look at his parents, but he didn't know if that was allowed, and he knew that if he did, somebody would start crying again.

"So, Sawyer," the ADA said, leaning back in his chair. "You play basketball?"

Did he? Should he? Sawyer hesitated, glancing over at Ms. Dixon.

The ADA laughed. "It's not a trick question. I just want to be sure you know what I mean when I tell you that the case against you is a slam dunk."

Behind him, Sawyer heard a sob.

"Uh, yes, sir. I know what that means."

"Good. That'll make this a little easier for all of us. Let's go over some of the evidence. We've got video of you breaking in, you inside with your little friend—here's a couple screen shots to refresh your memory."

Sawyer looked at the pictures for the hundredth time, Grace with her beret, him too stupid to pull down his ski mask. Not that it would have mattered. The printouts were grainy and overexposed. The clips from the video that they'd been showing on the news were better than these.

"We've got you coming out the door. Obviously. Oh, and you're the one that did that bit with the soap. You're lucky nobody got hurt. Or worse, knocked into one of those statues. We'd be having a different conversation if they had. We've got video of the guards falling on their butts," he said, chuckling. "It was pretty clever of you."

"Thanks," Sawyer said, before his attorney's hand pressed against his forearm and he remembered to shut the hell up.

"Now we come to Miss Grace Sherman. How well do you know her?"

Sawyer looked to Ms. Dixon, and when she nodded

he said, "I guess not all that well."

"See, that's another thing I don't understand. You've only known this girl, what, a couple of months? Less? Now, I can see if she asked you to give her a free ice cream or sneak her into the movies, but breaking into a museum?" He shook his head. "According to your attorney, you're not romantically involved with Miss Sherman, correct?"

"Yes, sir. I mean, we weren't going out."

"How about physically?"

"Well, we went places together—"

"Were you having sex?"

"No, sir. It wasn't anything like that."

The ADA shrugged. "Frankly, it would be easier to understand if it were. Anyway, about this first painting, the one you two stole from the Wood Library—"

"My client hasn't been charged in that case and he has nothing to say about it at this time."

"Right, right, no problem. Sorry. We can talk about it later," the ADA said, looking at a large color photocopy of *Moroccan Market* in the file. Somehow the paper copy made it look more expensive, like it *could* be worth millions.

"We found the painting hanging on the wall in Miss Sherman's room. Not like she was trying to hide it. The only thing on *any* of the walls in the whole house. You've been there, seen inside the place?"

Sawyer shook his head.

"How people can live like that, I don't know. Her room was different, but the rest of the house? Anyway, this painting. It's nice. Not my style, but there's something interesting about it." He brought the paper up close to his face, then held it out at arm's length before handing it to Sawyer. "Here, your eyes are better than mine. See if you can make out the artist's name on the frame."

Sawyer studied the picture, taking the time to read the small brass nameplate even though he knew what it said. "It looks like G. Ravlin."

"Yeah, that's it, G. Ravlin," the ADA said, then he looked straight at Sawyer. "*Grace* Ravlin."

It took a second, but the ADA got the reaction he was expecting, Sawyer's eyes going wide, his mouth dropping open.

"Heck of a coincidence, don't you think? I mean, Grace is not exactly a common name. Maybe it was in 1917 when that was painted, but now?" He went back to flipping through the folder. "I'd bet the odds of somebody named Grace *stealing* a painting by an artist named Grace—totally at random, without knowing in advance the name of the artist—well, I'd bet they'd be pretty darn low, don't you think?"

Sawyer knew that he was the one who had spotted the painting, that he had pointed it out to Grace. But then she was the one who had insisted that they drive twenty miles out of town to go to that library, that they work in that room, at that table, arranging it so that he sat in the one chair that would put *Moroccan Market* where he couldn't miss it.

The ADA flipped more pages, stopping now and then to read something he didn't share. "Grace Ravlin. Grace Sherman. That's a nice coincidence. Oh, and here's another one you might find interesting. It involves that photograph you stole—I'm sorry, you've been *charged* with stealing. Here's a photocopy of it from an art book the museum loaned us. Remind you of anybody?"

Of course it did. He had noticed it the first time he saw it—same kind of hat, same short haircut, same backlit eyes, that same knowing smile that was in her mug shot.

"The resemblance is uncanny. Not so much in the newspaper, but in person you can't miss it. That's probably what she'll look like in a few years. Very pretty.

According to the museum, it's a self-portrait of the artist. Any guess on the artist's first name?"

"Grace?"

"That would be something, wouldn't it? Both works of art created by someone named Grace, *stolen* by a girl named Grace? That's the kind of coincidence that makes you realize it's no coincidence. But that's not the case here. Nope, the artist's name is not Grace. It's Cindy," the ADA said, smiling at Sawyer. He paused, sharpened his smile. "Cindy *Sherman*."

The ADA had telegraphed it, swinging in wide like a roundhouse punch you saw coming but couldn't duck, and when it hit, Sawyer didn't move, didn't react, but his ears were ringing and his head felt numb.

"Let's recap, shall we? We have a stolen painting by *Grace* Ravlin, recovered in the bedroom of *Grace* Sherman, the same Grace *Sherman* who goes on to steal a photograph by Cindy *Sherman*." He slapped shut the folder and leaned in. "Sawyer, in my business, I've learned that there's no such thing as a coincidence."

The bottom of his stomach dropped out next, then his left leg started bouncing in time with his racing pulse. The ADA opened another folder. Sawyer saw his own name typed out on the tab.

"As I'm sure you and your parents recall, some police officers stopped by your house that Friday afternoon with a search warrant. They didn't find anything there that looked suspicious. Good for you. But your phone records and these texts"—he shook his head as he scanned a list of dates and phone numbers, every word of his text messages printed in sequence—"these won't help your cause."

He picked up a second folder, this one thick and worn, notes written on the outside and forms stapled to the back. A white sticker on the tab read SHERMAN, GRACE.

"The officers also searched Miss Sherman's home. Let's see. The painting you already know about. This other stuff." He raised an eyebrow but kept reading. "Information on the Wood Library, on the art gallery, bios on the artists, hand-drawn maps and floor plans. Quite detailed. Impressive. Lots of books. Here's a whole box of electronic gear, spy cameras. Celebrity magazines, *hundreds* of those. And best of all—what will probably be my Exhibit A—step-by-step detailed plans for both burglaries."

Grace's voice whispered in his head. *Don't mock my*

methods. Planning's the best part.

The ADA skimmed down a lined sheet of paper with block paragraphs written in tight cursive. "Sawyer, do you know a Vicki Alva?"

Sawyer thought for a second, then shook his head. "No, sir."

"Grace never mentioned her? Never brought up her name? Interesting." He read some more, then slipped the paper back in the folder. "This Vicki Alva, she's a long-distance flight attendant with United. Lives in an apartment on the west side, a small complex, eight units, back behind an old strip mall. We found her work schedule on Miss Sherman's computer. And we also found a key that fits the apartment. No idea how she got ahold of that. Anyway, the flight attendant is pretty upset, as you can imagine. Last week she found a diet cream soda in the fridge and she *knew* she didn't put it there. But she also says that nothing appears to be missing."

I gave her my word I'd be good.

"I'm sure there's a connection and we'll find it," the ADA said, fanning pages of the folder. "But what we don't have, Sawyer, is any connection to you. We've been through it all, the notebooks, the computer files.

You're not mentioned once. Not even hinted at. And we haven't found your fingerprints on anything we checked. Frankly, I don't think we will."

I would never rat you out. That's not my style.

"So you're admitting you don't have a case against my client."

"Nice try, Ms. Dixon. No, we have a great case. But that doesn't mean that I'm happy about it." The ADA leaned forward in his chair, folding his hands on his desk and looking right at Sawyer as he spoke. "I think you were used by a very clever, very resourceful young lady who got you to do what she wanted you to do. It was all part of her plan. Your attorney says you've only known Miss Sherman for a couple of months. Ask yourself, how did you two meet, what did she do to win your trust? You said it wasn't sexual. Fine. But somehow—and in a very short time—she got you to commit—"

"Allegedly commit."

"—a serious crime. Think about it, Sawyer. During that time, did she ever just *bump into* you somewhere? You think that was by chance? And those *casual conversations* you probably had? Trust me, son, there was nothing casual about them."

Yes, there was. Sawyer knew it, felt it deep where his heart used to be, as sure of it as he was of anything. But they would never understand and he would never be able to explain it since he couldn't explain it to himself.

"And I believe that if it wasn't you, it would have been somebody else. You were just a guy she needed to help commit these crimes. Who knows, she could have tried that act on a dozen guys, looking for the one she could play. And I'm sure that if you had said no, I'd be sitting here going through the same folder with some other guy."

No, he was wrong. It couldn't have been that way. There would have been no other guy. It would have been just Grace, the way she always wanted it, the way she planned it.

"You're a smart kid, Sawyer."

Wrong kind of smart.

"Honor roll every quarter."

Wrong kind of honor.

"Planning to go to Wembly in the fall."

Wrong plan.

"And she used you, and took it all away."

"I assume there's a purpose behind this buildup," Ms. Dixon said, her tone—polite, bored—making it clear what she thought of the speech.

The ADA folded his hands on his desk. "Miss Sherman isn't talking. Hasn't said one word about the painting in her room or how it got there, or said anything about the art museum or Sawyer's role in any of this. Not a word. Yet. But she will."

Sawyer smiled at that.

"This is not her first run-in with the legal system. I can't get into details since much of it occurred when she was a juvenile and those records are sealed, but suffice it to say that we're familiar with Miss Sherman. And her family." He turned and looked at Ms. Dixon, his tone changing. "There are other pending cases involving various members of the Sherman family, and while it's certainly not essential, it would be *helpful* to have additional weight to bring to bear on those cases."

Ms. Dixon leaned forward. "Complete immunity, and an ACD."

"That depends on what your client has to share."

"But if he cooperates and agrees to allocute in chambers?"

The ADA nodded. "That would work."

"Hold on," Sawyer said. "What are you talking about?"

Ms. Dixon turned in her chair. "A plea agreement. You testify against this Sherman girl—tell everything you know and admit your part in any crimes she may have committed—and the judge will give you an ACD. An adjournment in contemplation of dismissal."

"Basically it's a free pass. You stay out of trouble for six months, all the charges against you will be dropped."

Sawyer's father cleared his throat. "But what about the things he says in court? Can't they recharge him for those, uh, crimes?"

"No, he'd have immunity," the ADA said, then looked at Sawyer. "Nothing you say in court can be used against you. An adjournment in contemplation of dismissal is not a form of probation, it's not even considered a conviction. The six-month period passes and you stay out of trouble—and I mean *any* trouble—and it'll be like you were never arrested. The records will be sealed, no one will ever have to know."

More sobs behind him, but different this time, almost happy.

"What would happen to Grace if I don't testify against her?"

For a moment, nothing moved.

Then Ms. Dixon shifted in her chair, the ADA slumped back, and he could feel his parents' stare burning into the back of his head.

"We have a surefire case against her without you saying a single word. We have the videos and the physical evidence at the scene, plus what we found in her room. Plans, photographs, maps, lists of supplies, internet searches—everything neatly laid out. It's almost as if she knew she'd get caught. Even planned it that way."

Impossible.

Getting caught wasn't part of her plan.

"However, your testimony will enable us to show a pattern of behavior that has less to do with her than it does with the adult family members in her life." He sighed, and for a moment looked less like a district attorney and more like a father. "Listen. My goal is not to see Miss Sherman locked away forever. She's had a rough start in life and maybe she deserves a second chance. But for that to happen she needs to be held accountable for what's she's done. Now, I could push for more, but when she's found guilty—and she *will* be found guilty—I'll request a three-year sentence. She'll serve about half that. Maybe less. Then a few years of probation. What you should be asking," he said, looking straight at Sawyer, no trace of a smile on his face, "is what would happen to you. You don't take the deal, right now, you'll be charged and you will go to jail."

Throat dry, palms sweating, Sawyer drew in a shallow, choppy breath.

"This is it, Sawyer. Decision time."

I need you to steal something for me.

"You can either take the plea deal, testify against Grace Sherman, and get back your life—"

My word's all I got. And some diet cream soda.

"—or you can start planning to do jail time."

There's a word for people who make a lot of plans.

"Now, I don't understand your relationship with this girl—"

An umbrella relationship.

"—and I don't know what either of you got out of it—"

You gotta stick close together if you want it to work.

"—and I'm sure you'll feel guilty speaking against her—"

Disposable and one-sided, based on fulfilling short-term, self-centered needs.

"—but you have to start thinking for yourself."

Now, you ready for this?

"It's all up to you now, Sawyer. You testify against her or you go to jail. What's it gonna be?"

CHAPTER
38

SAWYER WAITED AT the door to be buzzed in.

He looked up at the security camera so the guard could see his face, see his uniform, and when he heard the buzz and the electric *click* of the lock, he pulled the door open and stepped inside. As usual, the hallway was empty, but he knew that there was a camera somewhere.

There always was.

Now, was there somebody on the other side of the camera? He had seen enough things going on in the hallways that went unpunished to make him wonder. Not that it would make a difference for him. They had made it clear where he stood when he started there, and he knew they were hoping they could spot one little infraction so they could nail him for it. There were days when he thought, *The hell with it, just do something and get it over with*, but this wasn't one of them.

There was a common area at the end of the hallway where a soundless closed-circuit TV played twenty-four hours a day, listing irrelevant schedule updates, week-old weather reports, inaccurate cafeteria menus, and other information nobody needed. There was furniture in the common area—padded benches and a row of chairs that looked like they came from an old bus station—but he'd never seen anybody sitting there. On the wall, next to a notice about this being a nonsmoking facility, screw holes showed where the pay phone used to hang, back when they had pay phones in the building.

Another hallway branched off from the common area. He knocked at the first door and listened. Overhead, the fluorescent light hummed. Inside the room someone was typing.

"What?"

"It's me," he said.

"Well don't stand there, come in."

He tried to turn the doorknob. "It's locked."

286

From inside he heard the pissed-off sigh and swearing he expected, a chair scraping against a tile floor, bare feet stomping across the room, and the deadbolt clicking back. Then the door swung open and Zoë stared at him.

"I *thought* I gave you a key."

"You did," he said, stepping into the room as she turned and went back to her desk. "But you also told me not to walk in without knocking."

"So knock, then use the key. It's not that hard to figure out." She shuffled some papers and tilted the screen of her laptop. "Great. Now I forgot what I was going to write. Thanks a lot."

Sawyer sat down on the edge of the single bed.

Kearney Hall was the oldest dorm at Wembly, with the smallest rooms on campus, but every room was a single, and if you went to Wembly and you were a female and didn't want a roommate—or if you had a roommate, several different roommates in less than a month, and you couldn't *stand* living with any of them and the administration was tired of dealing with you and your constant complaints—it was where you lived.

Unless you still lived at home with your parents, in the same room you'd been in since you were five.

Zoë's room was trashed, but he had stopped joking about it back in October, and by March he no longer noticed. The window was open and the blinds were down. They rattled with every late spring breeze.

Sawyer watched her type for a few minutes, then leaned over to check the time on the screen. "You going to be ready to go soon?"

"Do I *look* like I'm ready?"

She didn't. She was wearing pink sweatpants with *KKG* in white letters on her ass, and the oversized Odenbach beer T-shirt she slept in. Her hair was pulled back and held up with a clip. She hadn't showered, which wasn't a problem, but she wasn't wearing her uniform, either, and he didn't see it among the piles of clothes on the floor.

"I take it you're not going," he said.

"I have to finish this *stupid* paper for sociology. It was due Friday."

"What's it on?"

"Teenage alcoholism," she said, typing as she spoke. "Or eating disorders. I have to see where it ends up going."

"What about the game?"

"Just go without me. It's not like I'm any good."

It was true, she wasn't, but it was her sorority's team

and she was the one that insisted they sign up to play in the coed volleyball intramural league because it was going to be *so* much fun, even though it meant giving up his Sunday shift at Mike's Ice Cream and all the tips he would have made. It was supposed to be a social league, something free to do on campus, but no one had explained that to the other teams, each one of them with at least six varsity players on their rosters. Zoë's team had been out of the running since the third week, the last week any of it was fun.

"I should have picked a different major," Zoë said, Googling "beer" and "bulimia." "You haven't had to do a paper all year."

He had—several of them—but not for his major. Accounting was more about numbers, especially for those in the Insurance Actuary program. Eyes closed, he flopped back on the bed, pulling a pillow under his head. The team would have to lose without him.

"Drunkorexia?"

"It's ten o'clock on a Sunday morning," he said. "I haven't had anything to drink in hours."

"No, it's this disorder thing," Zoe said, reading the search results. "Huh, it's *real*. Excellent. Now I know what my paper's on."

"You found it on the internet?"

"Yeah, where else am I supposed to look?"

"It may not be real."

"There's like a hundred thousand websites about it. It's got to be. Here, check it out, a whole story on it. Just got posted on TMZ."

"Is that some sociology site?"

"Sort of. It's celebrity gossip and stuff." Her voice trailed off and he listened as she clicked and scrolled, and when she screamed, he jumped.

"Oh my god. It's *her*."

The way she said it—voice curling up, the word growing out—he didn't have to ask.

He knew who it was.

And he knew he had to look.

A headline, a small story, and that mug shot.

ART THIEF TEEN TO STAR IN OWN REALITY SHOW

She still has six months to go on her sentence, but studio execs at Pazajama Productions confirm that nineteen-year-old *fille fatale* Grace Sherman will star in her own crime-based reality series, *Grace Under Pressure*.

The show, loosely based on Sherman's own real-life

misadventure, will pit contestants against each other and the clock as they race to plan and pull off an art heist of their own. An empty shopping mall in northern Ohio will be converted into a make-believe museum, with reproductions of famous works of art standing in for the real thing.

Sherman first made news after she and a male companion were caught red-handed sneaking out of a museum with a priceless work of art. Prosecutors detailed the elaborate planning behind her almost-perfect caper, portraying the stylish high school senior as a criminal mastermind.

At her trial, the always-smiling Grace quipped from the stand that, while what she did was wrong, "it was a lot of fun."

The jury found her not guilty of the most serious charges, but a guilty verdict on minor charges earned her an eighteen-month sentence, bringing an end to the fun. At least temporarily.

Reece Denberg, spokesperson for Pazajama, said that filming will begin "as soon as Grace is available."

The show is slated to be part of the winter lineup on TLC.

Bits of half-forgotten conversations echoed in his head while he read, and bigger things, things he knew now that he wished he had known then, things about plans and dreams and Grace, falling into place, six weeks of his life replaying in an instant.

Zoë clicked on the mug shot until it filled the screen, the ice-blue eyes larger than life.

"Oh my god, can you *believe* that bitch? *Look* at her. I'd like to slap that smile off her face. Ugh, and that stupid hat. Why'd they let her leave that on? It looks ridiculous. And now the bitch is getting a show. I wonder who she had to screw to get *that*, the little slut. The show's going to suck anyway. Who's going to wanna watch *her*? At least they didn't mention *your* name. Thank god. They can't, right? That would be *awful*. People would think you were like *her*. And what would that say about me? Ugh, she makes me sick. What did you ever see in her, anyway? I know, I said I would never go there, but come on, look at her, she's freaky Westie ghetto trash. What were you thinking? You could have thrown your whole life away because of her. Did you ever think about *that*? Huh? Ever wonder where you'd be right now, what your life would be like if you had stayed with her? Well, do you?"

"All the time," Sawyer said, looking deep into the eyes on the screen, his vision blurring from the light.

THANKS TO—

PATTY, for casing the joint

ANNE, for coming up with the plan

MOLLY and **LAUREL,** for "fixing" the alarm

THE DIXON SCHWABL GANG, for the getaway

LIBRARIANS and **BOOKSELLERS,**
for fencing the goods

And to **TIM ARMSTRONG**
and **SKYE SWEETNAM,**
for the theme song.